THE AEROWYN TALES

# Bellarose

## AND THE

# Captain

## CARLA REIGHARD

*To those who feel worthless or unseen.*
*Your worth isn't based on what you see in the mirror.*
*Actions show who you really are—beauty or the beast.*

# Acknowledgements

The words 'thank you' aren't adequate for any of the magnificent
people I've met through this author journey:
Cathy McCrumb, the best editor for this book!
Jenn Phares, beta reader, encourager, and friend.

# Chapter 1

# Bellarose

B ella made her way past the brigantine's masts to the bow and gazed across the turquoise depths. Overhead, ropes and riggings creaked in the wind, which tugged on her clean clothes and pulled the ribbon from her hair. The stiff breeze mussed her brown locks, and she pushed a wisp out of her mouth. Bella raised her chin to breathe in the salty air. The exhilarating motion of whipping tresses matched the wild spirit breaking free inside her. The prim and proper girl with perfectly coiffed hair no longer existed. Her messy strands and sun-reddened cheeks mirrored her internal transformation.

No story in any book—however detailed—could ever come close to being entangled in those heart-stopping moments like the fantastical ones she had read about in fairy tales, moments when the world no longer felt safe. Although...

Bella bit her lip. While visiting Ageless Isle with its mythical creatures had been perfectly enchanting, most of those events were harrowing times she wanted to forget. She breathed out.

Nothing was mundane about the way the *Notre Dame* sliced gracefully through the water. Only an hour before this mesmerizing calm, a hurricane had wreaked havoc on the now placid ocean. Captain Modo had swum through the tumultuous waves to rescue her from drowning. No, her current situation was far from humdrum.

Bella wrapped her arms around her middle. For all its beauty, the ocean reminded her of the thing she wished to forget—how an exciting voyage to a new world became a path to misery.

She mentally replayed her conversation with Modo after he salvaged her from the sea. He was too formal and stated rules of propriety like she needed to be schooled. Recalling the captain's stern demeanor didn't prevent Bella from pondering his handsome face. He would be even more dashing if he smiled.

Ocean mist moistened her cheeks and playful dolphins splashed before the ship, sending more spray into the air. She chuckled to herself. If the austere captain could channel the dolphins' energy, then perhaps the journey back to New Orleans wouldn't be as long and boring as it promised.

At least the spectacular views wouldn't be monotonous.

Bella did want a calmer life, so perhaps the no-nonsense captain was exactly the sort of person who could return normalcy.

The wind carried Modo's scent of pine and a hint of something familiar along with the sound of his boots on the wooden deck. She turned to face him. Sunlight caught on his brown hair revealing copper highlights, and his warm brown eyes would have been comforting, if they hadn't reminded her too much of Quinn, the one she loved and lost. She quickly blinked away the tears.

Captain Modo's posture was impeccably straight as he strode to her side, a leather pouch in one hand. Bella tilted her head to meet his eyes, but when their gazes connected, he quickly looked away and cleared his throat.

"Miss Bonnay, may I tend to your wounds?" He gestured to his satchel. "I would have done so earlier, but it was important that you changed from your wet clothing first."

Bella looked down at her sore palms. "I would appreciate that. I'm surprised my room didn't do that for me after it did everything else."

Modo's brows raised. "What do you mean?"

"You would have to see it to believe it. I still can't comprehend fully, but you did say Aerowyn provided this ship for you and she is a powerful enchantress. Magic must be seeping from every board on this vessel."

"If you only knew the half of it," Modo mumbled while he led Bella to some barrels.

He set the bag on the closest container and pulled out ointments and clean bandages. She rested her hands by the medical satchel. Modo was surprisingly gentle, even though his palms were strong and rough. His touch sent a pleasant tingle through Bella, despite the discomfort.

Bella couldn't help but replay how he had effortlessly hauled her to safety from the turbulent ocean. The rescue reminded her of a story's damsel in distress, where deliverance led to real love's kiss. She quickly dismissed that romantic notion.

Captain Modo was a stranger, and nothing like her Quinn. She couldn't love a man who was too solemn. Quinn's fabulous sense of humor had made her laugh every time they spent moments together.

Modo's rescue confirmed another difference between the two men. Though Quinn was a master at sword fighting, his hunched back would have made it difficult or even dangerous for him to swim through the witch's squall. As much as she longed for Quinn to be on the *Black Fear* with her, the idea that Quinn could have died at sea horrified her. She shook the thought away and concentrated on the man bandaging her scraped palms.

"I noticed your hands when I hoisted you onto the *Notre Dame.*" Modo's voice was gentler than normal. "If the question isn't too personal, how did you manage to injure them?"

"When the storm hit, I grabbed onto the rigging to avoid getting tossed into the sea, but my hands were too slippery. Even when my grip loosened, the ropes yanked me across the deck and into the water. My palms were rope-burned, and I hit every hard surface before getting dunked. I'm bruised all over."

Concern etched Modo's face. "That tempest was unexpected and took us off course."

"How long will it take us to reach New Orleans?"

"I do not know. Since we are in a magical realm, my maps do not show these oceans." Modo finished wrapping her left hand. "Aerowyn told me she would keep our ship on the correct course and that once we reach territory on human maps, I would know."

"I anticipate the worst whenever the enchantress is nearby." Bella sighed in exasperation. "Callista—she's the sea witch who created the storm—hates Aerowyn and her father, Peter. It only makes sense that she tried to ruin the fae's designs with that squall."

"I wonder what plans they had before the storm ruined them."

"Other than the fae king's mission to rid the world of selfishness and cruelty, which has created creatures ten times more dangerous than their original selves, I honestly don't know." She shrugged. "But I always seem to be in the middle of Peter, and Aerowyn's schemes."

Modo's brows scrunched together like her words were disagreeable. "What do you mean?"

"Ever since a mysterious old lady in New Orleans told me where to find work on the plantation Aerowyn had enchanted, I seem to be embroiled in their plots. When Jasper Falcon kidnapped me, the fae king himself protected me from said pirate. Now, I find myself on a ship Aerowyn created to rescue me from that kidnapping? Why keep me safe from Jasper? Why send you to rescue me?"

"I see your point. I don't have answers for your questions, but it does seem the enchantress has pulled you into her plans." Modo's eyes darted to the side. "Anyway, please be careful what you do until your wounds heal."

"Thank you for helping me." Bella smiled. "I couldn't have managed this by myself."

Though he finished with her hands, he didn't release them right away. In a gruffer tone he replied, "It is a captain's duty to ensure all his crew and passengers are well. We do not have a doctor, but I know a few basics. I have had to dress injuries multiple times in my previous life."

"You haven't always been a captain?" She couldn't imagine him doing anything else, despite his apparent youth. "What did you do?"

"That is not important, Miss Bonnay." He let go of her hand. "How do the bandages feel? Are they too loose or too tight? They will need to be changed often until your rope burns and abrasions heal, to avoid infection."

"They're fine, thank you. But if we are to be friends, it's important to learn more about each other."

He squared his jaw and looked up, then, and his warm brown eyes were the only thing that seemed unguarded. Unless it was her imagination, they reminded her again of Quinn's. She looked down to avoid the comparison.

Despite having the same surname, Captain Modo and Quinn had such opposite personalities that it was absurd to think of the one she loved when in the presence of this stranger. The captain had already confirmed he was no relation to her Quinn. However, both men, evoked a stirring inside her. Bella quickly squashed it. She didn't need complications and heartbreak.

"As I said before, Miss Bonnay," Captain Modo's intimidating baritone reiterated, "we cannot be too familiar with each other. The crew would get the wrong idea about our relationship." The captain shifted his weight, almost as if he were uncomfortable. "I am not like Captain Falcon. I will not be making inappropriate advances toward you."

"I don't think being friends with me would give the incorrect impression." Bella stopped and added curtly, "But I do recall you telling me to address you by your title. I apologize, Captain, I forgot my place."

Without another word, he gathered the satchel and strode away.

Bella exhaled. She wouldn't mind a nice casual conversation to pass the time, but that wouldn't happen with Captain Modo. His inability to relax his guard made it hard for her to know how to understand him, and the excuse of shielding her reputation seemed unwarranted. It was going to be a tedious journey returning to Louisiana.

Directionally-challenged Bella asked several sailors the way back to her cabin and found it soon enough. The ornately carved door was her first reminder of what she had forgotten. She hurried inside and shut it, then drew in a huge breath and took in the surroundings.

Bella chuckled. "Why was I so worried about time dragging with the stuffy captain?"

Whatever else the fae did, Aerowyn knew Bella loved books when the enchantress had conjured the shelves full of volumes in Bella's quarters. The library contained everything she would need to spend the days in style.

Quick-passing visions of a place she couldn't recall visiting startled her. It wasn't France, her home country. Perhaps her wild imagination was leaking into reality. The pleasant décor seemed reminiscent of

Christmas-time—but the fact that she called the holiday Christmas instead of Noël made her second-guess the memory.

Wooden bowls of orange and clove pomander balls rested on the table, and pine garland draped the bookshelves.

The comforting scents made her quarters a respite, even though decorations shouldn't have been eerily familiar. In her Family French chateau, the servants put out more religious symbols for Noël and kept Yule logs burning in every hearth.

Determined to remain light-hearted and thankful, Bella forced herself to stop questioning the discrepancies of her recollections, pushing all the odd thoughts back into a compartment of unexplained occurrences, and skimmed the shelves' titles.

"Hmm... *The Princess Dragon* sounds intriguing." She grabbed the tome and settled into the nearby plush rose patterned chair to dive into a new adventure.

· — · ● ☀ ● · — ·

Bella ate up the tomes like a starved orphan would fresh bread from a bakery. Despite the way they took her to faraway lands where unsavory conditions stayed in the pages, however, she couldn't read for weeks on end. Even though a passenger, she wanted to pull her weight, so she begged the captain for busy work. Anything to do, from swabbing the deck to helping the cook cut vegetables. Captain Modo, however, forbade it until her wounds healed.

When her palms were finally free from blisters and abrasions, she found her way to the deck, where she spotted Jeb, a friend and former crew member of the *Black Fear*. She made her way aft to join him. No longer on a pirate ship, Jeb had grown almost unrecognizable from his former self. His normally greasy red hair was cleaned and combed. His usual sweaty body odor was less noticeable, too, for which she was thankful.

"Jeb," she called. "I need something to do. Would you teach me to sew?"

He hesitated. "I dunno, Beller."

"See?" She held up her unbandaged hands. "My wounds are healed. I'm ready to become a contributing crew member."

"Aye," he said after a moment's consideration.

Jeb led her belowdecks where he mended whatever the ship needed repaired. The men's personal items and hammocks made it somewhat claustrophobic. Once more, Bella struggled with the smells that brought back the memories of her parents' deaths. She pushed the sharp pain to the farthest recesses of her mind.

"Sit 'ere in me sew'n corner," Jeb's voice brought her back to the present. "The men know to leave it alone."

Bella sat, and Jeb proceeded to show her how to darn a sock. Once she figured it out, she pulled the basketful close and repaired several holes while they conversed.

"Beller, wha' ya fink of Cap'n Modo?"

Bella finished her last sock and picked up a shirt. "I'm not sure what to think about him. He's polite, but—"

"No, ya mus' use fis for shirts." Jeb handed Bella a daintier needle.

Bella tried not to stare at the dirt under his fingernails.

"Thank you. I know it must seem strange that I don't have a clue what I'm doing, but a long time ago I was a privileged baron's daughter who didn't do anything for herself."

"I was'n judgin'. You was sayin' the cap'n is polite, but..."

"He's too no-nonsense." Bella made a lopsided stitch and hoped no one would notice. "When he brought us onboard the *Notre Dame*, I was struck by the fact that she's named after the cathedral in Paris."

"Is she?"

Bella nodded. "*Notre Dame* means 'Our Lady'. I know ships are referred to with feminine pronouns, but to give one the same name as a church seems a little odd, even if it suits the captain's personality. He's formal... and distant and guarded. He reminds me of how I felt when Mère and Père took me to grand cathedrals in France."

"Who took ya?"

"My mother and father. It's what we call them in French."

"French? Oh, aye. 'At's why ya talk funny." Jeb cocked his head to the side. "Why ain't ye wif yer folks?"

"They died on the ship we took to America." Tears threatened to fall, so she blinked them away. "Even if they were alive, Jasper kidnapped me."

Jeb squirmed. "Oh, aye. He did. I'm sorry about yer parents and the nabbing. Cap'n Falcon was a pirate an' nothin' like Modo. But I do see wha' ya mean about the cap'n being a bit stuffy."

Bella stopped her stitching to look at Jeb.

"We're friends, right?"

He stopped sewing and gave her an earnest smile. "Yer like a sis'er to me."

"Then I can tell you that Jasper sometimes made improper advances to me. I know you admired him, but he wasn't a good man until he saved Cerise, the mermaid." Bella let out a huge breath. It was a relief to get that off her chest. "I'm thankful Captain Modo isn't like Jasper, but I wouldn't mind a little more conversation from him. I feel like he doesn't know how to relax or even smile."

"I don' know. 'E smiles all the time when 'e stares at ya." Jeb sniggered and waggled his eyebrows.

"Stares at me?" Bella laughed. "I've never seen that. He barely makes eye contact with me."

"When yer 'ead is turn, 'e looks all the time."

Warmth crept into her cheeks. If she was completely honest with herself, the thought of Modo being attracted to her was flattering. He was probably only eighteen or nineteen but acted mature beyond his years, capable of leading a group of men who were older than he was. How had someone so young attained such a prestigious position? Well, Aerowyn *had* used him to rescue Bella. Her thoughts of the enchantress led her to remember fairy tales. The fairy godmother had turned mice into horses and some other animals into footmen for Cinderella's carriage to the ball.

Maybe Captain Modo was a mouse.

She chuckled.

Jeb crinkled his eyes. "Wha' so funny?"

"I recalled a story about a fairy godmother who turned mice into horses." She grinned. "And, since Aerowyn chose Captain Modo, perhaps he was a mouse or cat before she changed him into a captain."

Jeb hooted. "Ya means ya fink 'e acts unusual because 'e's an animal?"

Bella giggled. "Yes."

Their laughter hid the sound of footsteps, and when the captain suddenly appeared before them, Bella's face blazed with heat.

# Chapter 2

# Captain Modo

C aptain Modo was looking for Bella to invite her to dinner when he found her with Jeb repairing holes in the crew's clothing. After he heard his name, a flash of insecurity kept him from revealing his presence. He didn't mean to eavesdrop, but curiosity got the better of manners.

She thought he was too formal? He was only behaving the way he assumed a proper ship's captain would conduct himself. Besides, becoming too friendly with Bella could cause him to forget they were supposed to be strangers, not friends from the past. Aerowyn's condition for his transformation was to keep his true identity a secret. Although he had always hoped for more than friendship with Bella, Aerowyn's spell should be the key.

Then, Jeb made a remark about him being an animal, and Bella snickered and agreed. Modo's temple pulsed. He was all man, not some rodent that would transform back to its beady-eyed self after the stroke of midnight as explained in the Cinderella tale. Maybe the ship and its crew would go back to inanimate objects or mice, but he was most definitely a man.

The jab cut deep, and flashbacks of his former life swam before him. Before Aerowyn's hex, he was treated like an animal—or worse, a monster. His stomach twisted. He wanted Bella to like him, but the mockery didn't only bruise his ego. Even worse, it risked the positive outcome he longed for. Would he still be treated like the beast even after Aerowyn turned him into the prince?

Modo clenched his jaw to push back tears and extinguish his rage to avoid being like his father. He stiffened his spine and stepped forward. He had to stop the path Bella and Jeb's conversation had taken.

"Sorry to interrupt your fun."

Mortification spread across Bella's features. "I..."

Her discomfort disarmed his anger, and his face heated too.

"I was wondering—" he coughed nervously "—Miss Bonnay, if you would like to join me for dinner tonight? I asked a few of the officers to attend, and the cook wanted to surprise you with something."

Bella's eyes darted between her mending and his face. She replied, "I would be honored."

"I will inform Finn that you will be joining us." Captain Modo pivoted on his boot heel and hurried away.

Sweat slid down his forehead, but he waited until he knew they couldn't see him before he wiped it away. It wouldn't do to have Bella see how nervous she made him even if it did prove he was a man instead of a rodent.

Avoiding the men on deck, Modo escaped to his quarters. The memory of Bella's lingering rose scent, replaced by the now-familiar aroma of oak and cedar. He drew in a deep breath to center himself. Late afternoon sunlight streamed through the windows of his captain's quarters, bathing the maps and navigating tools scattered across his desk. The tidy, wrinkle-free green coverlet was tucked tightly underneath his bed's mattress. His surroundings would have taken his mind off the girl, but the book, *The Scorned Fae,* taken rashly from Bella's library, reminded him of their time together before pirates and fae tore them apart. A lump formed in his throat. Returning to his cabin hadn't helped compose his emotions.

He attempted to ignore thoughts of Bella by organizing the maps strewn all over his desk, but when that didn't work, he grabbed his favorite sword and swished it through the air half-heartedly.

He had been a blacksmith in New Orleans, a trade learned at his father's command to keep him out-of-sight. However, the act of molding metal to form a blade always helped him sort through his feelings. When he wasn't creating swords, he practiced with the weapons he had forged and imagined he was a dashing captain aboard a mighty vessel. His dreams came to fruition, but was the price too high?

He put the sword back into its sheath frustrated by his encounters with Bella. He wanted more than polite conversation of instructions and queries, but if Bella figured out who he was, the consequences would undo everything. Bella didn't know he had previously been Quinn. To fulfil his deal with Aerowyn and find his own perfect ending, Modo had to keep his true identity a secret.

Gazing at the vast ocean, he thought of Bella's kindness in New Orleans. She brought out the best in him. He wanted nothing more than to be her hero, even if he'd never felt worthy of her attention or friendship.

All his life, people had feared and insulted Quinn because of his hunched back and had told him that he was worthless and grotesque. His father never truly loved him, but blamed him for his mother's death in childbirth. Quinn's only value was free labor.

No, he had never received compassion from another human being until Bella came around. The glares, grimaces, and ridicules were etched permanently inside his mind, even though Bella's smile imprinted on his heart. If he had summoned the nerve to share his true feelings with her, what would Bella have said? If she, too, rejected him, his heart would break beyond repair. He exhaled loudly.

When she ran off with that pirate and Aerowyn asked Quinn to rescue Bella, he had hesitated. Did she need rescuing? Modo clenched his fist.

Didn't it make sense that Captain Falcon had swayed her with the promise of riches and a better life? Jasper was dashing and dangerous. Isn't that the kind of man women were attracted to?

Despite his fears, his hand went to the letter he carried in his breast pocket. He knew the words by heart, but he pulled it out to reread it. Once more, a little hope soared inside.

*Dear Quinn,*

*I've decided to join Captain Falcon aboard his ship. Since I'm poor and don't belong at the plantation, Jasper has given me another option. I no longer want to be indebted to everyone and this is my opportunity to change my fate.*

*He told me that he offered you the same thing, and I hope you decide to join us. We leave tonight at midnight, and I'm already on the ship.*

*Sincerely,*

*Bellarose*

Jasper had offered him the job and when Quinn hadn't instantly agreed to join Captain Falcon's crew, he left without him. He thought Bella had decided to go regardless of whether or not he was on the ship. Quinn had doubted she had wanted him to join them.

His conversation with Aerowyn rose in front of him as if it had taken place only seconds earlier, morphing his captain's quarters into the stables where she had found him back in New Orleans.

*Aerowyn had stood there with the wolf, Gerard, leaning against her side. Quinn remembered him as an arrogant man Bella detested, but as a wolf he stood regally, though he had been humbled by the enchantress. She casually stroked the animal's head as she told Quinn that he must be the one to rescue Bella. His excuses came easily.*

"Look at me," he protested. "I'm no match for Jasper Falcon. She's probably already fallen in love with him. He has so much more to offer her than I have."

"You don't have much faith in her, do you?" Aerowyn's normally melodic voice sounded more discordant.

"What do you mean?"

Aerowyn sighed. "Do you honestly think a girl of her caliber would fall in love with a pirate without scruples? You should realize that is ridiculous. She's smart enough to see past his lies. She won't give into his charms, and you're a fool to believe otherwise."

"I do believe Bella will see past his gentlemanly act, but she told me she wanted to make her own way in the world and be independent of the de la Roses' generosity. Bella may not fall in love with a pirate, but she may be willing to change some of her ideals to better her situation. Her father was a baron. She's accustomed to the finer things."

Aerowyn's chocolate eyes turned violet. "Maybe you don't deserve her after all."

The change in her eyes and in her demeanor startled him. He clenched his jaw. He needed to tread lightly around the powerful enchantress. "I doubt anyone deserves Bella. She's a rare treasure. The thing is, I saw Gerard change due to Bella's influence. I was convinced she was falling in love with him because she went from loathing the man to admiring him." Quinn looked down at the wolf standing next to Aerowyn. "What if Jasper changes because of Bella, like Gerard did? She won't have any interest in me. She won't need saving."

Gerard made a slight throaty noise, and his ears pricked toward Quinn's voice.

"So, you're unwilling to take the risk?" Aerowyn inquired.

"I..."

The enchantress said coolly, "I can cast a spell on you to look like a capable debonair ship's captain. I'll give you a mighty ship and crew to rescue her, but ultimately you must be the one who saves Bella from her enemy. Your crew can't help in the rescue, other than manning the ship and getting you to where you need to go."

Hope and nerves made Quinn's hands shake. "And what will the cost of this spell be?"

"So, you are wise, too. When Gerard took Antoine's curse at the de la Rose plantation it must have shown you that magic has a price. If I transform you, the payment will cost you greatly. I can make you the most handsome man in New Orleans, but to make the enchantment permanent, Bella must fall in love with Captain Modo, not Quinn. If she doesn't, you will never                                    find true amour with anyone for the rest of your life. Your refusal to accept your value as you are now will turn my spell into a curse. If she had known you to be her friend Quinn, you would have a head start. No longer. She can't know you are Quinn Modo, the hunchback."

He glanced down at his calloused, large hands. "If I'm as handsome as Captain Falcon, getting her to love me will be easier."

Aerowyn harrumphed. "You have so little regard for Bella. She is attracted to kindness and selflessness above outward appearances."

Quinn Modo shook his head.

"What happens if Bella discovers I'm only Quinn, the tavern owner's son?"

"You return to the hunchbacked man."

He raked his hands through his hair. It was worth the risk to escape his ugliness. He didn't have love now, so what was the worst thing that could happen? At least if he was attractive, the insults and cruelty would stop.

*Even if Bella was attracted to kindness and selflessness, what had these traits ever done for him? Eye-catching men had whatever they wanted in life. An attractive face might make him vain like those men, but it didn't seem to prevent them from finding happiness. His only joy had come from knowing Bella, and if he didn't have her love, he would be content in the success better-looking men found.*

"Fine, I agree to your terms. I will rescue Bella. How can I get a ship and a crew?"

"I will take care of all of that. Remember: if you want to remain the handsome Captain Modo, you must be the one to save her. Come to the port at midnight and your journey will begin."

Aerowyn seemed to soften. "I know you are thinking of how Jasper Falcon also left at midnight."

*How had she known?*

"I should tell you that my father, Peter, pretended to be Jasper's first mate to protect Bella, but he can no longer help her. That is up to you now."

She held out a sealed paper. "This is a letter from Bella. My father was supposed to destroy it when Jasper asked him to kill you. She wrote this." She paused, then added, "Jasper kidnapped her."

"Jasper thinks I'm dead. What does Bella think?" Quinn clenched his fists ready to fight the pirate.

"That you didn't care enough for her to join their sea voyage."

"Did you ask her, or are you guessing?" *If Aerowyn's words were true, this made him despondent.*

"We fae have our ways of knowing, but it doesn't matter since you will no longer be Quinn. He might as well be dead, as far as you're concerned. If you decide to tell Bella you're Quinn, you will continue to be the captain of the ship I give you, but you'll look as you do now. You will still be able to rescue her and bring her to Louisiana safely."

Modo smoothed Bella's letter and tucked it back into his pocket.

For several minutes he stood looking out the large window at the aqua ocean laced with foam from the brigantine's passage.

He couldn't reveal who he was to Bella. If she truly thought he could be a hexed animal, it was nearly impossible Bella would give him her heart. Her rejection would confirm that he was unworthy of Bella, despite his appearance. It would be torture to only have her friendship, because eventually she would leave him for another man.

He couldn't accept Aerowyn's assessment of Bella's values. How could Bella love him because she admired his noble traits?

Whatever the outcome, though, he wanted to be rid of the hideous, maligned man he had always been.

# Chapter 3

# Bellarose

B ella was mortified. Her heart thundered while she shoved the needle in uneven stitches. Neither she nor Jeb spoke until Modo's steps had faded.

Jeb frowned.

"Do ya fink 'e 'eard us?"

"I don't know, but I want to hide in my room all night!" Bella dropped the needle and shirt to her lap. "I can't go to that dinner. I'll have to look at him and wonder." She pressed her palms to her face.

"Ya 'eard 'im say Finn is makin' somefin' special jus' fur you."

"I can't."

The former pirate tapped her shoulder, and she pulled her hands away from her face.

"Beller," he said, "ya 'ave to go."

"Oh, Jeb, I can't." Her shoulders sagged. "I know you—all of you from the *Black Fear*—have been my champions since Captain Falcon became a merman. You're almost like the brothers I never had. But I can't"

Jeb took the unfinished shirt from her and expertly finished mending the tear. "An' we wan' ya to be safe, but ya promised."

Once again, she realized she had underestimated the man. While their shared near-death experiences created a bond, he kept surprising her and helping her become less critical, not that she had shown that when she made that remark about the captain.

"But if he heard me..."

Jeb chuckled. "So, what if 'e did. Mistakes 'appen an' ya forgave others, so ya need to forgive yerself."

"Forgive myself for calling Captain Modo a hexed mouse?"

"Yes."

"Just when I thought I was becoming less judgmental, I go back to old habits. It was embarrassing and harsh."

"Don' worry. I got yer back and won' 'old a grudge."

He tucked the sewing supplies back in the basket, pushed himself to his feet, and held out a hand. "Come on."

Bella followed Jeb wordlessly.

He paused in front of the ladder. "I s'pose ya won' read tonigh' if ya eat wif the' cap'n?"

She smiled. "You all do enjoy the stories, don't you?"

"O'course. Af'er I tol' them yer leprechaun story, they wan'ed more."

Their requests had initiated nightly reading under the diamond-studded sky. After the crews' duties were completed, the men gathered on the upper deck to listen to Bella's narrations of magical lands, heroic princes, and fair maidens. It only took a few evenings for Bella to run out of stories she remembered or made up, so she began reading the volumes from her library.

"It's been my pleasure to read aloud," she confessed. "Maybe I should have dinner in my quarters so I can read to you all tonight."

Jeb didn't respond as he proceeded Bella up the ladder, and when they stood on the deck, he nodded toward the bow, where Finn was probably hard at work in the kitchen.

He scratched his jaw, then said, "'Member tha' one nigh' ya read abou' tha' wicked queen who was jealous of the pre'y girl?"

Still confused, she asked, "Snow White?"

"Yeah. An' when ya read the part about the queen disguisin' 'erself as an ol' woman offering the girl a pois'n apple, Finn said 'is mum 'ad an apple tree an' taugh' 'im 'ow to make the mos' delish apple pie?"

"Yes, of course I do," Bella replied. "I love apple pie. It seems like forever since I've had anything like that."

"Aye, then. Cap'n Falc'n didn' believe in spoilin' us with fancy food. But Finn said this ship got sugar, flour, fresh fruit, and spices. I laughed because someone tol' Finn to stop interruptin' the story so we could find ou' wha' happens to Snow White."

"And I continued to read." Bella's frown turned into a smile.

They reached her cabin and Jeb pointed at the ornately carved door.

"So, what you're saying is if even if I don't want to face the captain, I need to go and eat Finn's dessert, or he will be disappointed."

"Yeah. Now go on. Clean up. You've been hangin' aroun' wif an ol' sea dog all day."

Jeb left, and Bella resolutely stepped inside to get ready for Finn's treat—and dinner with Captain Modo.

Reluctantly, Bella stood, and the thought crept in again: why *did* the enchantress want her to be happy? The magical elements Aerowyn included in the room were evidence she wanted Bella to enjoy the voyage, but why?

As if the room read Bella's mind, sounds of water flowing from the tub along with the smell of rose-scented oils invaded her senses. An invisible force tugged on her dress, so as she learned, it was easier to raise her arms for the clothing to be taken off her body. Immediately, the discarded dress disappeared.

Bella gasped, but quickly recalled the message she saw scrawled across the room's mirror the first time it reacted to her needs.

*No one is in this room. Aerowyn enchanted all objects to anticipate and fulfill your every need or desire.*

Still thankful no people had been cursed as objects to serve her, Bella stepped into the warm bath water allowing the magical sponge to cleanse her. Aerowyn had created the room and all its comfort to make Bella's stay on the *Notre Dame* fantastic, but why? To coax her into loving life on sea with Captain Modo or something else?

# Chapter 4

# Captain Modo

M odo's smile widened when Bella came into the small dining area. The grin was a natural reaction—he couldn't stop even if he wanted to—but his words stuck in his throat. He hoped the two lieutenants present would help keep the conversation flowing. Though he wanted to prove he wasn't a prim no-nonsense captain, his former, isolated life had given him very little experience with socializing. Other than his friendship with Bella, contact with females had been minimal.

"Lieutenant Aerrol Flyntock and Lieutenant Gregory Butler, this is Bellarose Bonnay." They stood as Modo introduced them.

Aerrol was near enough to pull out the chair for Bella. "Even though we're officers, I don't think it would be improper for Miss Bonnay to call me Aerrol since she is a civilian. This is a long journey after all."

Modo blinked twice because he could have sworn the lieutenant's eyes changed colors as he spoke to Bella. That phenomenon only happened in one other person—actually a fae—whom he had met. No, it wasn't possible. He hurriedly dismissed the notion.

Bella flashed a smile. "And of course, you may call me Bella. All my friends do. I hope we can be friends, or this will be a lonely passage back to New Orleans." Bella gave Modo a look he couldn't decipher.

His other lieutenant's blue eyes sparkled with mischief as he bowed slightly. "I would like to be a part of your circle of friends. I'm Gregory." He waggled his eyebrows and Bella looked away with pinkened cheeks.

The way Gregory flirted with Bella reminded Modo of someone else he'd met in Louisiana, but that would mean... Modo ignored his suspicions. Jealousy twisted inside his chest, distracting him from anything but his insecurities, which niggled their way into his mind and defied his determination to not allow the suave officers to steal Bella's heart.

However, even after weeks under sail, he knew very little about these men or what their capabilities were. The whole ship and its contents probably dropped into thin air after Aerowyn had asked Modo to rescue Bella from the pirates. Maybe Aerrol Flyntock and Gregory Butler were magically altered mice. Aerowyn was an enchantress, after all.

Bella sat down at the table, and Aerrol gently pushed in her chair. Modo couldn't help but notice how the green in Bella's dress enhanced her emerald eyes. The clothes Aerowyn provided suited Bella perfectly, color and fit.

In the past, he always averted his eyes from women, only casting quick glances or sneaking unnoticed glimpses. Once Aerowyn cast her spell, however, Modo had the confidence to really look at Bella, and she was the most beautiful woman he knew.

Bella's eyes moved between him and the other men, and she nervously licked her ruby lips, distracting him from everything else.

All three were staring at him. Gregory had a mischievous grin, but Aerrol was scowling. Had someone asked him a question? Was Bella upset that he had overheard her conversation with Jeb?

Modo cleared his throat to speak before his silence made the situation more awkward. "How do you find your accommodations, Miss Bonnay?"

"Rather pleasant and magical." Bella fidgeted with the cutlery on the table and wouldn't make eye contact with him.

Before Modo could ask any more questions, the smell of roasted turkey with stuffing wafted through the air. Finn brought in the food, and the aroma made everyone at the table groan in delight.

"Finn, this looks delicious!" Bella flattered.

"Thanks! Just wait 'til the dessert." Finn's face reddened. "I made it special for you, 'cause of your stories."

Bella beamed. "I was told you had baked something special. I'm looking forward to it and I will certainly save room."

Finn backed out with an enamored look on his face.

Modo glanced around the table at the two handsome lieutenants, who stared unabashedly at the beautiful young woman. He was overwhelmed by the mission to win her heart, but apprehension trickled through him. He could lose her to these other men.

Was there anyone on this ship who wasn't infatuated with Bella?

# Chapter 5

# Bellarose

Modo was the least talkative person at the table, but Bella didn't mind, except that it seemed Jeb had been right about the captain staring at her. His attention, however, felt more like judgment than admiration. He probably thought she was a silly girl who enjoyed fairy tales. She didn't even have the skills to help aboard the ship.

Bella avoided eye-contact, but the captain's scrutiny made her restless and squirm in her chair. She wasn't the same vain, spoiled aristocrat's daughter from France. Her experiences had transformed her.

"Bella," Aerrol began, and her attention went to the young man to her left. His casual grin put her at ease. "I'm trying to place your accent. Where are you from originally?"

She ignored Modo's scowl. "The long story or short one?"

"Let's start with the short one since I don't want your food to get cold."

"I lived in France, but the story of how I came to America is long and less pleasant. I'd rather not discuss it now." Bella's throat tightened, but she contained her sadness at her parents' deaths.

"We did not mean to bring up tender memories." Modo gave her a sympathetic look that almost made him seem human rather than an emotionless object.

"Thank you." She glanced at the plate of turkey and sauce before she flashed a smile. "More recently, I lived near New Orleans. That's when Captain Falcon kidnapped me." Her smile faltered as her heart sped up at the memory, and she bit her lip. She'd feared she would die or be ravaged—maybe even both—before the journey had finished.

"That must have been dreadful for you," Gregory exclaimed. "And yet you survived."

"Yes, but that story would take longer to explain." Warmth flooded her cheeks. Even though Peter, the fae king, had kept her alive and her virtue uncompromised, these men must have been imagining the worst—that Jasper had his way with her. Didn't all pirate stories say they were cads?

Modo shifted nervously as everyone looked at him. His face turned pinker. Bella cringed. The first day he saved her from the sea, he'd assumed the same thing until she'd explained that Jasper's cursed, hooked hand had stopped him from doing anything nefarious.

Modo's deep voice squeaked slightly. "Perhaps the weather is a safer subject?"

Bella was taken aback. The stern man, old beyond his years, suddenly sounded like an insecure school-boy, which softened her heart toward him.

The two dashing lieutenants immediately complied with Modo's suggestion, and soon Bella was able to put her discomfort aside and resume her meal.

The relaxed sound of silverware clanking on bone china filled the room.

She ate until her stomach threatened to burst, but after the table had been cleared, Finn brought in his dessert and set it in front of her. Finn grinned as he stepped back.

The pie's flaky crust was golden to perfection with a light sprinkle of granulated sugar on top. Scents of cinnamon and apples made her mouth water.

"Finn, it looks almost too good to eat," she teased. "I have a confession. I knew ahead of time it was going to be apple pie."

"Who told ya?" Finn eyed the captain.

"I only told her it was a surprise dessert," Captain Modo protested.

"Jeb gave me the hint, but that was because I was thinking of skipping dinner. The pie convinced me to come here tonight."

Pain flashed over the captain's face, and Bella immediately regretted her confession. Bella swallowed hard, but quickly recovered when Modo's expression became unreadable.

Finn cut a slice and put it on a plate, then slid it in front of Bella and handed her a fork. "I'm happy the pie changed yer mind. Here, taste it."

Bella gingerly picked up a bite with her utensil while the whole table stared at her. She focused on the treat to avoid the men's attention and she scooped it into her mouth. Bold flavors exploded delightfully on her tongue.

"This," she gushed, "is the most delicious pastry I have ever tasted."

Finn's smile broadened, and his eyes lit up.

Her heart sank. She wanted a good rapport with her travel companions—especially the cook—but she didn't want anyone to fall in love with her. Maybe she was overreacting. Maybe he didn't exactly love her... but his expression was similar to Antoine de la Rose's when he looked at Brooke after his curse was broken and he was no longer a beast.

"Yes, Finn, that was a fine-tasting dessert." Aerrol smirked as the cook exited the room, still gazing at Bella and nearly running into the wall.

"I believe Bella has an admirer," Gregory teased.

Aerrol glanced at Modo. "I think she probably has more than one."

Every inch of Bella's skin warmed from mortification at the obvious reference to the captain. If hiding under the table wouldn't make her look foolish, she would scurry there immediately. She'd read of an invisibility cloak once. Maybe having one of those would have been even better.

Instead, Bella changed the subject. "I'm exhausted. I think I will retire early."

"Let me accompany you to your cabin." Captain Modo stood quickly and went to the other side of the table to pull out Bella's chair.

The lieutenants as well.

"Why should you get all the fun?" Gregory winked.

Bella needed to get away from everyone before she burst into flames from humiliation. "I'm perfectly capable of finding my room without any help. I'm sure as officers, you are all very busy."

"I have the time," the captain said. "I confess I'd like a little more conversation with you before the evening ends."

She bit her bottom lip. Would he confront her about her theory that he was a transformed mouse? She didn't seriously think he was cursed by Aerowyn, but it was too late to take back her words.

Protesting again would only draw more attention, so she stood.

Modo offered her his arm, and she was obliged to loop hers through his uniformed one. His muscles flexed under the jacket, and suddenly the idea of his large arms left her a little muddled on the insides.

Really, though, she had the same attraction to Quinn, even though he was always embarrassed by his humped back. Her upbringing valued perfect aesthetics over benevolence, but his kindness first drew her attention. Men who seemed physically perfect tended to be egotistical or vain. Of course, Bella's experiences with eligible men had been limited.

Both lieutenants bowed deeply, and the captain led her from the room and onto the deck where stars speckled the night sky. Captain Modo was indeed handsome, but in her opinion, Quinn had a supremely striking face. His chest and arms could never look like Jasper's or Captain Modo's, but she didn't care and wished he was here instead.

Her buckled shoe slipped on a wet spot, and the captain caught her, reminding her again of his strength. The memory of how he had rescued her and the way his shirt had clung to him gave her butterflies. She inwardly chided herself for allowing physical attractions to take over character. After all, Quinn did that to her without displaying massive muscles.

All the fresh ocean air was probably confounding her. It certainly didn't help that she was constantly surrounded by men all the time. She needed to clear her mind and stick to books. Although, even fictional men tended to be exceptionally attractive.

"A slice of pie for your thoughts." Modo's deep voice pulled her from that embarrassing line of contemplation.

Bella's heart raced. She would never share her admiration of any male's physique with the captain!

Quickly casting about for an appropriate response, she blurted, "Wouldn't having a conversation about my thoughts cross your lines of propriety? You don't want to call me by my first name, but you want to know what I'm thinking."

"I suppose I deserve some of your ire," he responded slowly. "I did not want to offend you by insisting you call me by my title. I only wanted to avoid Jasper's men thinking I would pick up where he left off. I am the opposite of that pirate."

"That is obvious to all," Bella said. But knowing the captain was attempting to offer an olive branch, she softened her voice. "I don't believe calling each other by our first names would give anyone on this ship the wrong impression. It doesn't matter one way or the other to me, but you are sending me mixed messages."

"What do you mean?"

"Do you want to become acquainted with me, or do you want to remain strictly the captain of this ship?" she asked quietly. "I doubt being friendly with me is part of your responsibilities."

They stopped by the railing amidships, and he stared out over the endless waves. "It is true I was given the role of delivering you safely to Louisiana, which does not include being your friend, but something you said to one of my lieutenants caused me to reconsider my stance."

"What was that?"

"You said it would be lonely if we could not be friends." He turned his gaze to her. "I was afraid to cross any boundaries, but I would like to start over with our introduction."

Confused by this man's flip-flopping opinions, Bella asked, "What do you mean?"

"You may call me—" Modo paused as if the words were stuck in his mouth, "Fitzwilliam. I am Fitzwilliam Modo."

"Oh, I didn't expect that."

His statement seemed inaccurate, and she scrambled for a reason why. While his hesitation made her wonder if he spoke the truth, she couldn't accuse him of lying. Surely there was no reason for the man to fib about his first name. She added hastily, "Then you may call me Bella."

"Glad we got that straight." He nodded solemnly. "Now, will you tell me what you were thinking earlier?"

In a flash, Bella recalled her begrudging attraction to this strange man. She raised her chin. "I wasn't thinking of anything that I want to share with you."

"That is an honest answer." He cocked his head. "If I can guess the topic, will you confide in me?"

"Probably not," she admitted.

He laughed lightly. "Again, you are straightforward. It is refreshing when so many people lie."

Bella's nerves jittered from Modo's desire to delve into her thoughts, so she tried a new tactic. "Why do you suppose that is?"

Modo pursed his lips. "The white lies we tell people to make them feel good about themselves probably seem innocuous, so we convince ourselves they are better than the truth. I suppose they are, but I think honesty can be achieved without sacrificing compassion for someone's feelings."

She studied him. "If a woman you found unattractive asked your opinion on her looks, would you tell her the truth?"

"I doubt any woman would do that." Modo frowned. "No woman would have asked when I was—" His hand trembled slightly. Was he nervous?

Modo continued, "In my previous occupation, women didn't seek my opinion, but let us say that—hypothetically—one asked. If I thought she was hideous, I believe I could be honest without hurting her vanity."

Her curiosity piqued, Bella prompted, "How?"

"I would say that beauty is highly subjective, and that she had an aura of beauty in the way she behaved."

Recalling her conversation with Jeb earlier that day, Bella frowned. "What if she acted atrociously and was mean-spirited?"

"I would tell her that even if her face enraptured a thousand men, her foul behavior made her odious to me."

Bella laughed out loud from shock, almost unable to believe how easily Modo presented the unfiltered truth. "You really would tell a woman that? It seems a bit harsh."

"I would, and it is." He shook his head. "Vain women become more hideous when people compliment their appearance. They tend to expect special treatment for their beauty, but I find beauty lies beneath the surface of a person."

"I agree. Not that I have a lot of experience with men trying to boost my self-esteem, but since my move to America, I have been confronted by men who were handsome—and they knew it. One man, Gerard, wanted me to dote on him like he was the most attractive of all men, but in my own way, I let him know he was odious to me."

Modo laughed so hard his face reddened. "Oh my, I now see another reason why so many men are smitten with you." He took her arm again, and they continued their walk. "Of course, you are beautiful, which is what your name means if I remember my French correctly, yet your feistiness and ability to say what is on your mind is really what wins their attention."

Bella was taken aback, and her cheeks flushed for what seemed the hundredth time that night. She attempted to ignore the compliment. How could he find her beautiful after what she had said about him to Jeb? Wasn't that exactly the behavior that made a woman hideous? Perhaps he hadn't overheard their conversation.

"I don't think so. If men do find me attractive, it is because I'm the only girl aboard this ship, so they don't have anyone to compare me to."

"I'm not sure that is true." His amusement settled into a smile. "You have won them over in ways you probably do not even know. It is easier to love a person who is selfless and compassionate over a self-centered, brutal person with a magnificent face."

"Yes. I had thought I had met someone like that, but..." She trailed off, afraid to show too much of her heart.

"But what?" he asked gently. When she didn't reply, he pressed, "Are you going to finish that sentence?"

Modo looked genuinely curious, so Bella drew a breath and admitted, "He turned out to not care as much for me as I cared for him."

His curiosity settled into a scowl. "Who is this fool?"

"No, please. I don't want you to think badly of him if you are ever introduced to him. You will be staying in New Orleans after you bring me back. You could meet him."

"Did he always live in New Orleans, then, or was he on the ship you took to America?"

"I met him at the first place I worked before the plantation."

"Where was that?"

His warm eyes coaxed it out of her. "I met him at The Swan. His name is Quinn, and he's the tavern owner's son."

Captain Modo turned his head away.

She continued, "Before you ask, The Swan was the local pub where I attempted to be a barmaid. I wasn't suited to that job." She looked down to avoid a disapproving expression. It wasn't one of her proudest moments. "I don't want you to think he was a fool for rejecting me. He has a hard life. Perhaps he didn't know my true feelings. It's possible that was why he didn't try to rescue me."

"Did this Quinn know you needed rescuing?" Modo asked earnestly.

"No." She sighed and made herself meet his eyes. "Captain Falcon forced me to write him a letter that asked him to join me aboard the ship where we both could escape our less-than-ideal circumstances, but even though I didn't tell him I was kidnapped by that pirate, I thought he would join us. He didn't. I wasn't worth the risk."

An unreadable expression came across Modo's face.

"Whatever his reasons were, I doubt he thought so little of you. Either way it was his loss but our gain. Of course, he was only one person. Could he have been able to get you away from the pirate if he had come along?"

"I don't know. Jasper lied to both of us about his true motives, so probably not. It was all for the best anyway, because I suspect the attempt might have killed him. Even if he isn't part of my life, I'm glad that he's safe."

They arrived in front of Bella's quarters. A lantern outside the door reflected light on the captain's face. Did he look... nervous?

In an attempt to put him at ease, or perhaps to coax Modo out of his shell, Bella said, "Thank you for the lovely dinner and talk."

"It was my pleasure. If you need anything, do not hesitate to ask."

"One more thing." Bella's stomach twisted in knots, but she had to know. "Did you hear my conversation with Jeb before you invited me to dinner?"

Modo coughed. "Um, well, yes I heard part of it."

"What part?"

"I must take my leave, goodnight, Miss Bon—I mean, Bella." He pivoted and left.

Bella knew she had been too brazen. She shouldn't have asked.

# Chapter 6

# Aerowyn

Lieutenant Aerrol Flyntock scanned the dining area and then whispered, "I thought they would never leave."

As the lieutenant spoke, black hair lengthened and transformed to blonde. The blue, formal uniform morphed into a lavender dress. Gone was the broad chest and in its place a slender curved female form.

Aerowyn blew out a breath and continued quietly. "I needed a break from that shape."

Lieutenant Gregory Butler beamed. "I'm happy to be a man again even if my face is slightly less handsome."

"I hope you're teasing, Gerard, because the glamour I used was perfect. If Bella wasn't meant to fall in love with someone else, she would find her attraction to my creation of the lieutenants hard to ignore."

"Yes, I will have to be careful, or she'll fall for me instead of—"

"Don't get too comfortable in your current form. You will go back to being a wolf as soon as we're finished here. I don't want you interfering with what needs to happen with Bella or Captain Modo." Aerowyn pointed at Gerard. "Unfortunately, your curse can't be broken by me. This is only a temporary glamour hex."

Gerard growled. His wolf was still at the surface. Despite the spell to make the beast appear as Gregory Butler, the animal was loosely restrained. "Why can you turn me into this man, but not back to my normal self? Haven't I proven my selflessness yet?"

"When you took your brother's place to lift the magic from the plantation, it... it changed things." Aerowyn's response was inadequate, and she knew it. The curse was beyond her power to reverse, and she was afraid to admit her failure. Tenderness—and fear—for Gerard bombarded her usual apathy. Eventually she would have to tell him the truth.

Gerard shrugged and said, "I'll accept that for now, because I know you care about me. You can't deny it." He flashed her a toothy grin and grabbed the last of the apple pie. "I don't know about you, but I'm still hungry. Maybe it's the canine in me." The aromatic scent of cinnamon and cooked apples lingered, even after the pastry disappeared into his mouth.

Gerard mumbled around a mouthful. "This is so good."

"Please show some manners," Aerowyn said, but her attempt at haughtiness fell flat.

The more time she spent with the oaf-turned-wolf-turned lieutenant, the fonder she grew of him. She wished she didn't think it, but he was adorable in all stages. Plus, his sacrifice for Antoine, his brother, had already chipped away at her original disdain for him, although, she didn't want to admit that her ice-cold heart was thawing to anyone, including herself.

Aerowyn was falling in love with Gerard—stuck in a wolf's body—and it was her own fault.

Gerard gulped down the last bite, "Sorry. Again, I think the creature has changed me." He used a cloth napkin to wipe the crumbs from his lips and asked, "Why are we here in these disguises anyway?"

"I didn't fully trust Modo to do what is needed so that Bella can have her happily-ever-after."

"If you want that guy to be less awkward, you should let me teach him a few lessons on wooing a woman." Gerard winked at Aerowyn.

Something fluttered inside her.

She had to get a grip on her emotions. This wasn't supposed to happen to a fae of her experience. She'd been in the world far too long.

Oblivious to her muddled emotions, Gerard continued, "Why does Bella need her happy ending anyway?"

"The more I learn about my father's curses the more questions I have, but I think Bella's perfect ending will help fix all the stories. Villains like Callista and Jasper shouldn't have existed."

"What does that mean?" Gerard leaned against the table.

"When Father traveled to other dimensions, he learned that the stories in those books Bella loves so much had different outcomes. He hasn't confessed everything to me, but I believe he has overused his powers and some of the hexes we've cast are creating worse outcomes than if we had left the cursed to live out their selfish lives."

Gerard frowned. "Does that mean my brother and I shouldn't have been cursed?"

"I hear Finn coming," she lied to avoid having that discussion before she was ready. "We don't have a good reason for lingering here."

His attention darted to the door. "My dog ears don't hear anything. Are you trying to avoid the question?"

"Maybe, but we don't want to risk getting caught," she said, and within seconds the enchantress was Aerrol Flyntock once again.

Gerard puffed out, grabbed the last piece of bread from the table, and gave Aerrol a jaunty salute before leaving the room.

They had to continue their roles as officers on the *Notre Dame* until the enchantress felt it was safe to leave Bella to discover her true love.

By then, perhaps Gerard would become a man again, and Aerowyn could find her own happily-ever-after.

# Chapter 7

# Captain Modo

More than anything, Modo wanted another chance with Bella. He'd foolishly thought he could manage a casual conversation with her, but how did he come up with the name Fitzwilliam?

It didn't matter, though, because instead of continuing the conversation, he ran away like the spineless creature he had always been. He paced his quarters. He had been lying to himself that if he looked as good as the war hero, Gerard or the roguish pirate, Jasper, she would love and respect him.

Yet, he had admitted to Bella that he was more impressed with how people acted than how they looked. Bella had the same opinion and admitted to caring for someone in New Orleans—for his former self, Quinn. Oh, the irony—the man he didn't want to look like—had earned her favor, and his new self, Captain Modo, had yet to figure out how to win her heart.

His breath hitched. The revelation bewildered him. She actually cared for Quinn, his former ugly, deformed self? That was impossible. Someone with her beauty and grace couldn't care for a beast. Aerowyn said he didn't deserve Bella if he thought her so shallow, but she deserved better. An aristocrat's daughter, who had her choice of suitors, wouldn't be able to marry a man like him, of zero financial and physical worth.

Modo continued to amble about in his cabin.

How could he get her to fall in love with him without deceiving her? He didn't want to be artificial, but who was he, really, without either his malformed back or his abusive father? Even though he knew the negative aspects of his past shouldn't define him, sometimes he clung to them. He wanted to escape, but in a hideous way, the abuse had become... comfortable. He was accustomed to hate. The thought that he was worthy of love was a little frightening, even though it was what he had always wanted.

He paused. Did other people hold on to their past hurts, or was he the only one?

Modo gave himself a shake. He had to reinvent himself, but how absurd it was to expect Bella to love him when he didn't even know who he really was? Maybe it would be best to leave Bella alone to find a better man—one more deserving of her love. He wanted Bella to be happy the rest of her life. He would rather love her from afar than make her miserable with a fraud like he was.

His body slackened at the thought of giving up so easily. As joy was sucked out of him, his energy plummeted. He wanted to curl up on his bed and sleep until he woke up from this nightmare. Everything Quinn had ever dreamed of having, Modo currently had, but he was miserable.

Aerowyn's words, "Be careful what you wish for," made more sense to him now that his wishes had been granted.

He stopped in front of his small mirror. Quinn's brown eyes stared back at him—granting him the courage to decide. No matter how many times his father's abuse gave him reasons to give up, he never quit.

He wouldn't quit this time, either. Bella was worth every ounce of determination he had. He would sleep on it and wake up with renewed vigor.

In the morning, he would try to talk with Bella again, to win over her heart.

Despite his resolution, Modo slept poorly, waking throughout the night from horrifying dreams in which Bella was kidnapped by the sea witch, who tried to kill all of them in another conjured hurricane. He woke with a new goal. Instead of wishing for time to woo Bella before returning to Louisiana, now all he wanted to do was distance her far from any monsters that could hurt her. He needed to deliver Bella safely to New Orleans before worrying about winning her heart. There would be time once they were safely on land.

Modo washed off the stress-induced perspiration before dressing with extra care, determined to be the dashing captain he wanted Bella to think he was. To his surprise, when he exited his quarters, he caught a glimpse of Bella herself. He turned and noticed her exasperated expression lift in a sigh of relief.

"Captain Mo—I mean, Fitzwilliam," she said blushing. "I'm thankful you're here. I'm lost! I'm looking for the galley, but I keep ending in the same place. I know I'm directionally challenged, but I should have this ship figured out by now."

Modo inhaled her delicately rose-scented presence. "I can show you the way. I wouldn't doubt the enchantress made it difficult to navigate for her own entertainment."

Secretly, Modo wondered if Aerowyn was forcing Bella to rely on him for help by tricking her into getting lost in front of his quarters. With the enchantress, nothing was off-limits.

The worried lines between Bella's brows smoothed out immediately. "Thank you."

Modo took the shortest route to lead Bella to her breakfast. He would rather have walked at Bella's side, but the passage was narrow. He couldn't steal glances to read the unspoken words on her face.

"Fitzwilliam is such a long name," she commented from behind him. "It's almost as formal as Captain Modo, and my tongue trips over it. Did anyone ever shorten it to Fitz?"

Modo's muscles tensed. The one simple lie about his first name would eventually lead to multiple falsehoods. How could he build a relationship with Bella if the foundation was based on deceit?

Even so, he fibbed, "My friends do."

She paused. "Hmm, I suppose that wouldn't be proper for me, since we barely know each other. Maybe I should stick to calling you Captain, or even Modo, so we're somewhere in between formal and familiar?"

"If you must." After all, he had thrown the fictitious name Fitzwilliam at her last night, so it made no sense to tell her not to. His realization that he needed to get her to safety prompted him to add, "It probably won't be an issue, since my duties will keep me busy."

They progressed toward the scent of bacon and warm bread.

Prior to entering the galley, he paused. "Speaking of duties, I know Jeb gave you some menial sewing responsibilities, but you are under no obligation to work aboard my ship. You are a lady of fine upbringing and—"

She set a hand on his arm to stop him. When he turned in the narrow passage, she lifted her chin and said, "I'm no longer that baron's daughter and refuse to become haughty over my lineage. Jeb is my friend, and I enjoy helping him with what you call menial tasks."

"Miss Bella, you misunderstood me. I only want you to be comfortable. I don't want you to feel obligated to earn your way as a crew member when you are more of a guest."

"I am comfortable helping. I want to feel useful and not spoiled."

She edged past him and headed toward the aromas, but before she entered the galley, she turned to say, "Thank you for assisting me."

Modo bowed. His own breakfast would have to wait since he had only managed to bruise her ego rather than put her at ease. She clearly didn't want to be told what she could or could not do to contribute during the journey.

Any progress he had made the night before had been thwarted, because of a difference in perspectives. This was not the girl he became acquainted with while teaching her to fight with a sword. He couldn't help but second guess his decision to become Captain Modo rather than remain her friend, Quinn.

It still seemed impossible that he would gain her undying love as Quinn did, but she would have been more patient with him. He pushed that doubt aside and clenched his jaw. No, her behavior was probably due to all the time she had spent traveling with pirates and magical fae.

Discouraged and hungry, Modo left Bella to her opinions and found his way to the upper decks. He gulped in a large amount of the briny air and allowed his muscles to loosen up. How could he accomplish what the enchantress enabled him to do? How could he—

"Cap'n?"

He almost jumped at Jeb's interruption.

"Cap'n, would it be alrigh' to have Beller practice sword play?"

Modo studied Jeb through narrowed eyes. "Did she ask if she could, or was it your idea?"

"She asked me."

Modo frowned. "I left her only minutes ago at the galley."

"Yeah, and I was there. I was done, but stuck aroun' to talk wif her. That's when she asked."

Jealousy nipped at Modo. This sailor spent more time with Bella than he did. "I don't know if we can spare you. Perhaps I could show her a few skills."

Jeb scratched his head, clearly puzzled. "Yes, Cap'n, but she says you tol' her to do wha'ever she wanted and that you prob'ly won' be see'n much of her."

Modo straightened and stared down at the former pirate. "I said you are needed elsewhere."

"Yessir," Jeb muttered before scurrying aft.

As the man scrambled away, Modo decided he had been too hasty in his decision to be busy. Despite the way he had angered her at breakfast, despite his duties, even despite the necessity of getting Bella safely to New Orleans, he would teach Bella as he had before.

He would give her a reason to like him if it was the last thing he did.

# Chapter 8

# Bellarose

After breakfast, Bella tried to find an alternate way to her quarters. She wanted to avoid Modo because their conversations always left her muddled. She couldn't explain why she got so angry with him earlier when he was only trying to put her at ease. She didn't want to be a burden to anyone, and he had only tried to explain that she wasn't.

Bella begrudgingly liked Modo. She refused to be vulnerable again and end up with another heart-break, as she had with Quinn, but it went deeper than that. Allowing another man to replace Quinn would feel like a betrayal. Her stomach twisted in knots whenever she tried to make sense of her illogical emotions and inhibitions.

She climbed down another level, hoping to find her cabin, but when she came upon some chickens, Bella knew she was way off her destination.

Her room was somewhere above the chicken coup, so she climbed up and wandered down a narrow hallway until she finally arrived at the easily identifiable, magnificent door to her quarters. The wood had been magically carved to look like shelves of books. She sighed with relief. She was in the right place at last.

Her room was as clean as ever, the bed smoothed and the wardrobe tidy. After a large breakfast, she wanted to read a little before looking for Jeb, who said he'd be willing to teach her swordplay in case they faced more pirates or sea monsters. While she remembered some of what Quinn had taught her, the longer she didn't use the skill, the rustier it became, and it was possible that her muscles were weaker from disuse. She missed the blade Quinn had designed for her that he kept stored in his blacksmith barn. It was lethal but light, and it would have been easier to use for her practice time with Jeb.

Pushing aside thoughts of Quinn, she grabbed a book and sank into the comfy reading chair inside her quarters. Whenever she did this, she saw another era where the bookshelves were more colorful. Were they from a dream? Whenever it happened, it left Bella confused. Each time the vision flashed she saw a girl, Layney who looked similar to Aerowyn, introduce her to a library in a future time. She shook off the memory as a dream where her mind confused stories and reality.

Her normal escape into books was not working and did little to assuage her discontent. She closed the tome with a sigh and stood. It wasn't fair to take her frustrations out on people who hadn't put her in the current situation. Modo hadn't been suggesting she live like an overindulged baron's daughter, but that she was free to if she wanted to. She crossed the room to track him down, but when she turned her cabin's doorknob, Modo was walking stiffly toward her like a plank was rammed up his back.

His demeanor set her on edge, and Bella cringed. She had been quite rude when she ended their last conversation, but his snobbish manner made it easy to forget her previous resolve to accept that he wasn't the enemy.

He gave her a stiff bow. "You're just the person I wanted to run into."

"What do you need?" Bella asked curtly.

"Jeb asked if he could train you in swordplay." He paused. "I believe I am more equipped to teach you than he is."

She crossed her arms over her chest. "Do you think I'm too good for Jeb?"

"Not at all." The captain shook his head. "Only that I am more skilled than he is."

"How would you know? Have you ever fought with him?"

"I saw his technique when we attempted to take over the *Black Fear II* before the storm did the job for us. He is brutal enough, but a clever opponent could trick him."

Of all the insufferable... Bella glared up at him. "Are you saying he's dumb because he's from a poor background?"

Modo blew out through tight lips. "No, that is not what I'm saying. Is that what you think I meant earlier? Let me get something straight. As I tried to explain to you before, I did not mean to imply you were too good for anyone on this ship. I reiterate, I only meant to ease your conscience of any guilt you may have of not contributing. Women do not normally perform daily tasks aboard a ship, and as I said this morning, you are a guest."

She almost accepted his explanation until his comment about women. "I see nothing wrong with a woman wanting to help out and share the load, but your comment about my upbringing sounded more like a command than an offer to assuage my conscience. As if you think I'm only supposed to look pretty and read books like *royalty*."

"You are putting words in my mouth." Modo's veins bulged, and for a second, Bella thought the marble captain's façade would break. "You are obviously too stubborn to believe my explanation no matter how many ways I attempt to relay it."

"I am not stubborn!"

He opened his mouth, closed it, turned, and left.

"Well, *someone* is acting like a stuck-up boor," Bella exclaimed loudly to his retreating back.

She spun, skirts flaring, and let the heavy door bang shut behind her.

# Chapter 9

# Captain Modo

How *dare* she twist his words?

Modo slammed his cabin door and paced the room in long, angry strides. He didn't know what his problem was. As Quinn, he'd been beaten down like a mangy dog. He'd found a smidgen of joy and confidence with Bella, who brought out the best in him, but now that he was handsome, she was bringing out the worst. Modo raked his fingers through his hair.

Frustration, confusion, and anger battled for the upper hand. True, his lack of experience with basic human interactions caused him to say things awkwardly and people misunderstood. However, Bella's reaction flustered him. His inadequacies in social etiquette never bothered her when he was Quinn.

He stopped midstride. Who was he lying to? It wasn't his stunted social life that made him speak rudely to Bella. He'd been mimicking the behavior of handsome men observed in his father's tavern. And it hadn't helped a bit.

The fact was, he wanted to become a new person. The chances of her discovering he had been Quinn were slim. He couldn't imagine her reaching the conclusion Quinn had been altered by Aerowyn, but if Bella figured it out, he was doomed to be Quinn again. He must keep this form. He needed to get Bella to fall in love with the new him. But what *did* Bella look for in a man?

Quinn Modo had always worked through problems with physical labor. Something about exertion cleared his brain. He changed out of his formal uniform and into more suitable clothes. His reflection caught his eye, and the increasingly familiar shape held his attention. When he was growing up, he avoided any reflections of his deformity—even in puddles. The more Modo admired his new, chiseled body, the more it became an addiction. Yet now his self-praise was turning into self-doubt.

He puffed up his chest and squared his jaw. Yes, that was his own self, looking back, confirming that Aerowyn's powerful spell had transformed him. Would it be enough for Bella to love?

He snatched up his blade and stomped to the stern where he would have space to expend his anxious energy. Several crewmen were attending to their duties, including Jeb, who was swabbing the deck. Modo's jaw clenched. He studied the former pirate through slitted eyes—jealousy boiling over Bella and Jeb's friendship.

"Jeb."

The red-haired man looked up.

"Come spar with me. Yes, I told you to do other tasks, but I've changed my mind. You may teach Bella to protect herself, if you can show me that you have the proper skills to do so."

"Aye, Cap'n." Jeb beamed with eagerness.

Jeb handed the mop to another sailor, and someone gave him a sword. Before the former pirate had a chance to find his footing, Modo swung his blade at the smaller man. Jeb jumped backward. Without much care for safety, Modo attacked again.

Lunging, parrying dodging, countering. The raucous clang of metal on metal quickly attracted an audience. From the corner of his eye, Modo recognized that Lieutenant Gregory Butler joined the small crowd.

Modo's blade nicked Jeb's arm, and he dropped his sword. The blade clanked onto the deck as a red line seeped through the rip in Jeb's shirt. He gritted his teeth and bent to pick up the weapon.

Gregory called out, "Captain, would you like to spar with me instead?"

Modo lowered his weapon and blinked at Gregory while Jeb slouched against the mizzenmast, breathing heavily.

The lieutenant stepped forward. "Is something wrong Captain?"

Modo shook his head. "No, I was caught up in the match. Bella wanted to learn how to defend herself, and Jeb was going to teach her. I was showing him some pertinent skills and assessing if he was up to the task."

Gregory leaned in and whispered, "It seemed more like you were attacking an enemy than training a subordinate." He said out loud, "Why don't you fight with me for a while and let Jeb learn from observation?"

Modo nodded his head. The sweat-drenched Jeb moved aside to make room for the officers to spar. It didn't take long until Modo's jealousy once more surged, this time because of the overly good-looking lieutenant. He was ready to conquer Gregory in an attempt to prove he was superior. Before their swords made contact, Bella entered his peripheral vision.

She gasped. The sound distracted Modo long enough for Gregory to gain the advantage and knock the weapon from Modo's hand.

"Jeb!" Bella exclaimed. "What happened?"

He reddened and pulled his arm away from the sailor who was wrapping a cloth around it. "Weren' nuffin', Beller," he muttered. "Me 'n the cap'n was practicin' wif swords, so's I could teach ya a coupla things."

Bella spun to face Modo, scorn evident on her face. "What do you think you're doing?"

"If it is not obvious, then you have more to learn than I originally thought." The words flew out, unintended, but Modo didn't let himself flinch.

The sun reflected off the clear aqua water forcing Bella to squint angrily.

"You know what I mean. First the cut on Jeb's arm, and then that murderous look when you faced Gregory."

Modo paused. Sails slapped in the breeze and he was thankful it dried his brow as he struggled to regain his composure. "I didn't mean to hurt Jeb." He straightened. "Since you wanted Jeb to teach you how to fight with a sword, I needed to see if he was skilled enough."

"Well *Quinn* never accidentally injured me whenever he trained me." Bella jutted out her chin defiantly. "I think you could have avoided it too."

Modo's heart sank. She told the truth.

"You're right." He slouched a little. "Jeb, my apologies."

The man nodded.

Modo's breath hitched. "It is not an excuse, but our earlier misunderstanding disconcerted me."

Bella's mouth dropped. "I was coming to apologize, but when I saw Jeb's cut..."

"I suppose we both have behaved badly."

Her lips lifted in a small grin. "We keep finding ourselves starting over again with each other. I say we stop letting our pride get the better of us. Do you want to shake in agreement?" She held out her hand to him.

The water lapping against the ship's side was the only sound. Modo was thankful that the sun and exertion would be blamed for his red face rather than discomfiture. He hesitated. His cruel behavior was more than pride, but he wasn't going to pass up a chance to make amends with Bella. He reached out and gently shook her hand. A tingle went through him from their touch.

She was all he had ever wanted in a woman.

Whatever happened, he vowed to become the man she deserved.

# Chapter 10

# Gerard

G regory smirked as the interaction between Bella and Modo unfolded. The poor naïve captain was trying to be something he was never raised to be. Gregory suspected Modo got all his education on how to interact with women from observation at his father's pub. The Swan wasn't a great place to learn how to woo a proper lady like Bella.

Even though she was kind, she could be stubborn.

Maybe the sword fight and injuring Jeb would do what Gregory's flirting hadn't—force Modo into action, though Gregory-who-had-been-Gerard harbored the tiny wish that Bella would fall for him instead. Not because he loved her, but because Bella had turned him down so many months ago in Louisiana.

Gregory gave himself a shake. That sort of petty desire for revenge could very well be the reason why Gerard was still cursed. Pride lingered, or perhaps, he was taking advantage of the situation. It was good to be a man temporarily, even if the face he wore was not his own, because he could practice being humbler. Perhaps Modo's example would teach him a thing or two about meekness, and he could show the captain lessons on confidence.

While Modo and Bella continued their low conversation, Gregory silently encouraged Jeb and the other sailors to go back to work and give the captain and Bella space. The two seemed oblivious to the small group dispersing. Gregory stayed within earshot of the conversation to report back to Aerowyn, but he pretended to be absorbed by the ocean's mesmerizing blue hues. It wasn't much of a pretend, though, because the colors reminded him of Aerowyn's ever-changing eyes.

The wind pushed a stray hair out of his neatly leather-tied queue and carried both the briny smells of the sea and the low murmur of Modo and Bella's voices.

Gregory tucked the hair back behind his ear. Those two were meant for each other, but the captain had made a mistake allowing Aerowyn to change him into an attractive young man. Bella really did like Quinn, though it had always perplexed Gregory how the girl gravitated toward the imperfect. Quinn thought his physical disabilities prevented him from rescuing Bella, but Aerowyn would have given him some magical help if he had remained in his own body.

Eventually, Modo took Bella's arm and walked away, but Gregory stayed to watch the water sparkle. From his own experience, it sometimes took living through Aerowyn's spells to understand what he really needed. At some point Modo would come to the same conclusion: he was better off as Quinn. Though, perhaps Bella would fall in love with Modo, and Aerowyn had promised Gerard that their happy ending would lead to his own.

Then, he could finally kiss the enchantress and tell her what was in his heart.

# Chapter 11

# Bellarose

M odo's touch warmed Bella's hand, making her wonder how it would feel to hold on longer than a brief handshake. His chocolate-brown eyes held her gaze without making her uncomfortable. They reminded her of Quinn's.

"I'm a little embarrassed by my appearance." Modo broke their eye contact and straightened his shirt. "I had better change. May I escort you somewhere before I return to my quarters?"

An odd sense of disappointment struck Bella that he didn't want to linger a few more minutes, but she forced a smile. "Maybe I will do a little reading before the mid-day meal. Thank you for the offer, but I can find my way."

He bowed slightly. Bella walked away in the direction of her cabin but glanced back to see him looking after her. She blushed and quickly turned her head away. It was strange, but his dishevelment reminded her of Quinn when he labored in the smithy forming horseshoes and blades.

"What are you thinking," she chided herself, "comparing Quinn and Modo once again?"

She needed to move past Quinn, to open her heart to other possibilities. He hadn't cared enough to join her. There was no point in pining. But, if Modo was disassembling the formal walls he had built around himself, perhaps there was hope for the future, despite his earlier display of temper.

While she made her way back to her cabin, Bella thought about her bookshelves. Maybe there were stories about dashing sea captains rescuing young maidens from pirates and broken hearts.

She chuckled to herself. Her rescue hadn't been quite that romantic. But if it had been… What if, instead of all the squabbles, he'd kissed her after rescuing her from the typhoon?

Her insides jolted as she visualized his lips on hers, their arms wrapped around each other in their sea-drenched clothes…

As Bella skimmed the shelved tomes, it happened again—a brief vision of another library. Unsettlingly dissimilar, like from an altogether, different era, disconcerted her. It was probably a misremembered dream. Bella returned to the books. Although she had only read half of them, they were not as she recalled. The familiar childhood fairy tales had twisted endings, with odd villains unexpectedly popping up.

Bella perused almost every book for one that could capture her attention. After pulling a dozen off the shelves, she settled down to read, but put them back. They weren't what she was in the mood for. Her eyelids drooped slightly. Maybe she should rest for a moment…

- · — ☼ — · · -

A soft meow and gentle pressure on her legs nudged Bell awake. She yawned and blinked blearily, then did a double-take at the orange tabby cat rubbing against her legs. She picked up the friendly, purring cat. A tagged collar around its neck caught her eye, so she tilted to read the cat's name.

"Hobbes? That's a good name." She rubbed his ear. "There weren't any cats aboard the *Notre Dame*. So where am I, sweet-face? Did the enchantress move me somewhere else?" A fog partially lifted from her memories as she studied Christmas decorations similar to the ones in her cabin. Again, that flash of another era and library were in front of her. This time it was a real place rather than a dream.

The cat purred and leaned into her palm.

"Am I on the ocean or somewhere else?" She chuckled and stroked Hobbes under his chin, then kissed his head. "You aren't going to be able to tell me anything."

Evidently finished with affection, Hobbes jumped onto a nearby plush chair and set to work licking his paws. Her attention drifted to the round table between them. Cookies piled on a snowflake-shaped plate beside a steaming cup of... What was that? The creamy scent seemed familiar. Had she tasted it before?

"Am I too trusting if I sample that treat?" Hobbes didn't answer, but Bella laughed.

Bella took a bite, and the cookie practically melted in her mouth. Flickers of the truth seeped into her head. *She was in another time and place.*

In another magical library in the real world. Her new neighbor, Elayne, had shown her. Elayne! Had she left her here?

"Layney," Bella called, "where are you?"

Hobbes stopped licking, gave her a contented look, and resumed his grooming.

"Why am I asking you? You're not a fairy tale animal that talks."

Hobbes purred loudly.

Glancing around, Bella noticed there were no doors—only walls of bookshelves. That triggered another memory.

Bella palmed her head. "I remember!" A lump formed in her throat. "I was trapped in this library."

Panic turned into action, and she began pulling books off the shelves hoping one of them would open a concealed passageway. She needed to escape the library and its fairy tales that forced her to participate in them.

"What are you doing?"

The familiar voice came out of nowhere.

Bella spun around. Her friend Elayne stood near the Christmas tree, arms crossed, brow creased.

"Layney, where have you been?"

"I've been inside those books." Layney pointed to the shelves. "Bella, there's no time to waste. Gerard and Quinn will be trapped inside the stories forever if we don't finish your tale."

Bella lifted her hand to her chest. "What are you talking about?"

Layney grabbed Bella's arm. "There isn't time to explain. You must return to the *Notre Dame*."

"No." Bella yanked her arm away. "I'm not going anywhere until you explain to me what's happening."

"I will, but you must come with me first," Layney pleaded.

Bella shook her head.

"Fine. It doesn't matter." Layney took out a stick—no, a wand. "You won't remember any of this anyway."

Bella's world turned black.

Hunger pains stirred her awake. Bella glanced at the gold clock on her nightstand and blinked. It was past supper time and she had obviously missed the midday meal as well. The beautiful clock played music at the top of the hour, but evidently the subtle tunes hadn't disturbed her sleep.

Bella stood and smoothed out her rumpled dress. An enchanted brush fixed her mussed curls. As she was about to leave in search of something to eat, a knock sounded. She jumped a little.

"Miss Beller?" Jeb called. "Are ya a'righ'?"

She opened the door to see Jeb's brows furrowed in worry.

"I'm fine." She yawned. "How is your wound?"

"It's fine." He put his hand to the spot that was bandaged. "I've 'ad worse, but wha' about ya? Ya miss' midday meal, but I fought it was Cap'n's fault. When ya miss' supper, I began to worry."

"Captain Modo and I worked out our differences. I came back here to read, but got a little sleepy. I thought I only rested my eyes for a short time, but clearly it was longer. Is there any way I can get something to eat? I'm starving."

"I'm sure Finn wouldn' min' fetchn' you somefing. He's infatuated with ya."

Bella groaned. She wasn't in the mood to deal with Finn's feelings. "Never mind." Her stomach grumbled in disagreement. "Maybe I'll eat a piece of cheese or slice of bread. I don't need him to prepare anything."

Bella shut the door behind her and followed Jeb to the galley.

"So, why'd ya 'ave trouble concentratin'?" he asked over his shoulder.

Bella wasn't ready to talk about whatever was going on between her and Modo. Her conscience twinged over forgetting Quinn so quickly.

She sighed, "I don't know. Maybe I'm tired of being on a journey I would never, never have chosen. I'm even tired of being on a ship. I'm ready to get on dry land and have some female conversation."

Jeb's shoulders sagged, and he said nothing as he ushered her into the galley, nodded respectfully, and left.

"Bella!" Finn smiled. "I missed ya—I mean, I'll gets you somethin' to eat."

He disappeared and returned with dried meat and cheese for Bella. "What's wrong with him?" Finn nodded toward the direction Jeb exited.

"I hope I wasn't short-tempered." Bella bit her lip. Had she accidentally bruised Jeb's feelings? If she had, she would need to apologize. "I think my adventures at sea are finally taking their toll. I never volunteered for this trip and am ready to be back in Louisiana."

"I suppose for someone not born to be a sailor; this can be too much ocean. I gets achy when I'm on land too long. I gots to be on water."

"It's probably a good thing there are people who like to be on ships. How else could we find transportation to other lands or receive rare goods if no one wanted to sail?"

"Exactly." Finn gave Bella a huge smile. "But... what if you fell in love with a sailor? Would ya like the sea then?"

Recalling Jeb's comment about Finn's feelings, Bella sighed loudly, hoping to warn the cook away. "How many wives travel with their husbands on ships?"

"None that I know, but if I was married, I'd want her nearby. Ain't no one gonna steal my woman."

Bella ate, but another empty ache took hunger's place. She'd been willing to call a ship her home—when she'd thought Quinn would be with her.

"Bella," Finn said, and she glanced at him. Finn smiled widely. "Have you ever been in love?"

"Only once with a man in Louisiana."

He frowned. "Is that why yer so eager to return there?"

"No, he doesn't care for me in that way."

Finn's crooked grin returned. "It's his loss. Ya knows, ya may not love me, but I would keep ya well fed."

Bella pursed her lips. "Oh Finn. You deserve someone who will love you. I'm not that girl."

His face dropped, but he stiffened his back. "I think yer the most beautiful girl in the world."

"But I'm not the right one for you."

"I'd quit sailn' if it changed yer mind."

"That wouldn't be fair. And it's not what love is all about."

"Love is sacrifice." He sat down across from her. "I'd do it for ya."

Footsteps sounded behind Bella, and both she and Finn startled. Finn's face reddened, and Bella turned in her seat.

Modo stood by the door. "Finn, could you fetch me some apple pie? I've been craving a piece since dinner."

"Yes Captain."

Finn scurried away to get the dessert.

"While you're cutting me a slice, go ahead and get one for Bella too." Modo called to Finn. "I don't want to eat alone."

Bella let out her breath slowly. Modo had rescued her once again. Her muscles relaxed, and she gave him a grateful smile.

The cook brought two plates of apple pie, then disappeared, and the clanking of pots and pans resumed.

Bella's eyebrows furrowed. Was he afraid the captain had overheard his proposal? Jasper would have boxed his ears. Maybe Finn wanted to steer clear of admonishment—or worse.

"When I didn't see you at supper time, I worried. I was headed to your quarters but ran into Jeb, who told me where you were."

Bella covered her face with her hands and then peeked at Modo. "It seems I am indebted once again to you for rescuing me." She laughed nervously. "I don't mind the interruption of an awkward marriage proposal."

"So, Finn finally summoned the courage to tell you how he feels." He shook his head. "Everyone saw the way he acted around you, but I didn't know he could be so—"

"Assertive?" she whispered so Finn wouldn't overhear. "Brazen?"

"Perhaps. I would not judge you if you wanted to marry him. He does make delicious food." Modo's faint grin disappeared. "But I think all the crew struggles with how to feel about you. Miss Bonnay, you have made quite an impression on my ship. Um, it seems no matter what I say, I never know exactly how to act around you."

She raised her eyes from her plate. "Why is that?"

"I haven't been myself since I boarded this ship." He grimaced. "What I want to be versus how I act contradict each other."

Bella crossed her arms and asked, "Did Aerowyn..." She paused and glanced at the galley. "Did Aerowyn cast a hex on you too?"

Modo averted his eyes. "I'm not allowed to say."

"Is that because Aerowyn told you not to or because you're afraid of the consequences if I find out the truth?"

"You can come to your own conclusions." Modo stood. "Before I say too much or something that you could misinterpret, I'll bid you goodnight."

"I didn't mean for you to leave." Bella jumped to her feet and reached across the table to touch Modo's arm. "Sometimes my bookworm curiosity takes over the etiquette lessons my mother taught me.

I always want to know the next part in the story before I'm supposed to."

Modo sat facing Bella. "Do you think this is part of a story?"

His expression seemed open, unguarded, like a child excited to learn new things. He appeared genuinely curious to know her opinion, which made her feel valuable and safe. She was automatically drawn to innocence over worldliness—someone open to possibilities over someone who was jaded and shut down.

"Actually, I was only comparing our odd relationship, or whatever it is to one in a book. Sometimes I feel as if Aerowyn is directing my life, like a play I can't escape performing." Embarrassed by her theory, she fidgeted with her fingers.

The captain picked up his fork and cut into the pie's flaky crust. As he chewed, Bella took a bite, if only to avoid staring at him. The sweet taste of fruit and spices offered a pleasant distraction while she waited for him to respond.

Modo swallowed. "I'm interested in what you mean about Aerowyn writing your life like a play. Um, I've had a few of my own questions about the enchantress's motives, based on my dealings with her, and I think you may be on to something."

"Really?" Bella gulped loudly and her face grew warm. "You don't think I'm a silly girl who has read one too many fairy tales?"

"I've never thought that." Modo gave her an adorable, crooked grin.

The expression was so like Quinn's that Bella suddenly felt comfortable, so she leaned forward to share more of her theory. "Aerowyn and her father seem to involve me in other peoples' lives, but each time they say they want me to be happy and safe. Why is that?"

He took another bite and chewed slowly. Bella pushed bits of the pie around her plate as she waited for his response.

Finally, he said, "I don't have an answer for you. Has any of what they involved you in made you happy?"

"Losing my job at the tavern and getting stuck with an arrogant jerk wasn't pleasant."

"I assume neither was being kidnapped by a bloodthirsty pirate."

She shook her head. "It wasn't."

Bella smiled and Modo gave her a questioning look.

"I guess the happiness came after their lives changed," she explained. "Although I've been in the middle of horrifying circumstances, the enchantress has provided me with extra pleasantries."

"Such as?" he prompted.

"My cabin on this ship is a perfect example."

Modo nodded. "That library is wonderful."

"It isn't only the library." She beamed. "Did you know the room is enchanted to wait on me like my own personal maid? Did you see the tub? It fills with water automatically. The clothes I wear disappear and are replaced with new ones. Invisible hands brush and style my hair."

"What?" His eyebrows rose. "I don't believe it."

She stood. "I'll show you."

Modo finished his last bite while she waited, then Bella took the lead. When she turned left instead of right, he gently steered her the other direction.

"The room even tidies my clutter."

"I'm not quite sure I believe you."

Bella looked back at Modo.

He offered her a partial smile and amended his statement. "It's true we've had some supernatural occurrences on this journey, but you have to admit the idea of a self-cleaning room is a little far-fetched."

She huffed. "I'll show you."

Modo stopped abruptly at her door. "This is too intimate. I still need to be the proper gentleman."

Bella sighed in exasperation. "We'll leave the door open. No one will believe you'll take advantage of me when anyone could walk by and catch you in the act."

Modo's cheeks reddened, and for a moment she thought he might burst into flames from embarrassment. He took a half-step backward into the hall and gave her a slight bow. "Even so, I will take your word for it. I shouldn't have doubted you, not after all we've encountered. I respect your judgement and know you speak the truth."

It wasn't what she would have expected, and for some reason, Bella's senses twirled, like when he'd bandaged her wounds. This man angered and dazzled her all in one day. He backed up another step.

She bit her lip and asked quietly, "Why do you do that?"

"Do what?"

"Back away from me anytime I get close physically or emotionally."

"Um, I'm the captain. I can't be—"

Bella closed in the space between them quickly and kissed his cheek before he could finish. The sensation of his evening stubble under her lips sent tingles through her body. The captain took a huge step backward, like someone had physically shoved him against the wooden bulkhead.

The blood rushed from her face, leaving her cold and boneless as a jellyfish.

Modo stared at Bella as if he'd been bitten by a viper, pivoted, and hurried away.

Dumbfounded by her own actions, Bella froze in the doorway. She could have heard a pin drop.

# Chapter 12

# Captain Modo

M odo dashed down the narrow hall, feeling as if the floor were going to drop out from under him.

She kissed him!

He came to a stop, and his fingers brushed over the spot her lips had touched.

She kissed him, and he fled like she was some kind of pariah. Bella would probably never give him any more chances.

What had he done?

Appalled at his actions, he hurried past a couple of sailors, reached his room, and shut the door tightly behind him. A huge rush of air escaped his lungs, and he slapped his palm against his forehead in punishment for his stupidity.

"What an idiotic fool!"

How would he ever be able to explain his behavior now?

Why did he have to react so horribly to the only time any girl had ever kissed him? To the only time *Bella* had kissed him? The memory of her soft lips on his cheek, made his body buzz. Why did he leave her? Why hadn't he kissed her back? Or even bade her good night? What if he had lost his chance at his own happily-ever-after?

He caught a glimpse of his reflection as he paced, but instead of granting him satisfaction, the handsome face brought him to a stop. The truth was, he realized with a start, that he didn't want Bella's attention because of his outward appearance. He wanted the kind of love that looked past his face or body—a love that connected souls. The kind of love that accepted the person he was yesterday, today, and in the future. Was that even possible as long as he hid behind his reimagined body? Because she could never know he was the Quinn she had loved.

He stepped closer to the mirror and studied the features he knew better than the ones that he was born with. Since Aerowyn had erased his ugliness, pride battled with humility, but he was still Quinn Modo. The beaten and downtrodden boy still lingered within the confident, debonair ship's captain. Everyone had seen the inner fight when his temper had flared that afternoon and he could have killed a man. Quinn wouldn't have done that.

His shoulders slumped. It didn't matter. He had repaired his relationship with Jeb, but Bella... What was done couldn't be undone. He'd utterly ruined any bridge between them the moment he ran from her. Even if Bella had started to care, she wouldn't now.

A rapping on his door pulled him out of his self-deprecating inner dialogue.

"Captain. It's Lieutenant Flyntock. May I come in?"

Modo straightened and masked his emotions. "Yes, Aerrol, you may."

The door opened. Aerrol Flyntock grinned while holding aloft a dark brown bottle and two glasses. "I heard about what happened with Gregory and Jeb, and then Bella's interference. I thought you might like a drink."

Aerrol clunked the glasses onto the round table, popped open the cork and poured. The sounds reminded Modo of his father's tavern and how it changed gentler men into angry ones.

"No, Lieutenant, I do not partake in drinking spirits. I need to keep my wits as a captain. Besides, Bella and I had worked things out until…"

"Until what?"

"Nothing. It doesn't matter now." Modo struggled to keep from showing the anguish his reactions to Bella had caused.

Aerrol raised his eyebrows. "You look like things still aren't settled." He lifted the tumbler of the brown liquid to his mouth and gulped it down. "Have a drink and relax a little."

"I don't need to relax like that." Modo frowned at the glass of what smelled like rum, which he knew pirates like Jasper imbibed, but not him.

"All right, if you're not going to enjoy a little rum with me, then I'll be on my way. I suspect being a ship's captain with such high standards can be lonely." Aerrol turned to face Modo. "I don't think letting your guard down a little would be improper when it comes to Bella. She isn't part of your crew and you catch more unicorns with honey than vinegar."

Before Modo could reply to the lieutenant's borderline insubordination, the other man vanished from his room. Modo blinked. Was he imagining things? The door didn't squeak. Had he hallucinated that strange encounter with Aerrol Flyntock?

No, the lieutenant had left a shot glass behind. It only held a small amount of rum, and although Modo had never tasted the stuff, his curiosity overran his sensibility. He stuck his finger into the brown substance and licked the wet tip. The droplet barely burned, but gulping the spirits would be like setting fire in his throat. The taste wasn't appealing at all, so Modo was thankful he hadn't sampled more.

Even so, his eyesight blurred, and the room spun. Modo stumbled to his bed moments before his leaden body collapsed. He managed to move onto his back. The rum must have been... poisoned.

The dreamless oblivion swallowed him into its blackened depths.

# Chapter 13

# Aerowyn

Lieutenant Aerrol Flyntock left the captain's quarters with a smug expression and hurried to the room where Lieutenant Gregory Butler waited.

"Are you going to tell me why you drugged poor Modo?" Gregory asked.

"I wanted to give him some peace of mind before all his self-loathing thoughts made him do something drastic. He's going to have an opportunity to redeem himself once again in Bella's eyes."

A confused expression washed over Gregory's face. "I thought Bella and Modo had finally made amends."

"They did, but then—never mind." Aerrol sighed. An explanation would require knowledge of magic Gregory didn't have. "Since he didn't want to drink any of the hexed rum, I had to cast another spell to make him curious enough to taste it."

"How much would he have to sample to pass out?" Gregory inquired.

"Only a finger-tip full." Aerrol held thumb and forefinger to demonstrate. "Even Modo wouldn't feel improper for tasting such a small amount. Now enough on that topic."

Pulling a golden scepter from thin-air, Aerrol waved it and changed back into Aerowyn. Her lavender gown flared as she inspected her body. Everything was as it should be.

Gregory's lips curled upward. "Now that's better."

"Don't get too comfortable. I only needed a short break from being in that form. It really is hard to act like a man."

"You're better looking as a woman." Gregory winked.

Aerowyn rolled her eyes. "Enough of that. We need to be serious. Father has asked me to return to Ageless Isle through our mental link, but we need to stay on the *Notre Dame* a little longer." She smoothed her dress. "I have an uneasy feeling something is going to happen to Bella."

Gregory's cocky grin turned downward. "What do you mean? Is she in danger? She's not going to die, is she?"

"I don't think she'll die, but I suspect we're being watched. I doubt we've seen the last of Callista." Her stomach clenched at the thought. "I could be wrong, but my senses are normally accurate.

"Let's hope you're wrong this time."

She had never been before, but she didn't argue. It wouldn't help to cause him unnecessary worry. He had obviously grown fond of Bella despite their shaky beginnings.

Aerowyn cared more for Gerard's mental well-being than she wanted to. She didn't know when she had stopped thinking of him as a mission and began to view him as a man, but maybe if Gerard ended up with his happy ending, she would too.

# Chapter 14

# Captain Modo

The raucous sound of drums woke the captain out from his drug-induced stupor. The ship's violent shaking almost threw him from his bed. Modo searched his groggy memory. Was the rhythm 'beat to quarters' or all hands on deck?

His ears rang—or was it the boatswains pounding the alert? Modo squinted into the sunlight flooding through his windows. He grabbed his jacket and tripped over his sword on his way to the door. The ship jolted again, and a man screamed.

"Cap'n Modo!"

Modo flung the door open. Jeb's pale face and knitted brows greeted him.

"Cap'n. Yer needed above."

The men raced to the stairs and clambered to the upper deck.

For half a second, Modo froze.

Large, spikey, black tentacles slashed at his crew from over the brigantine's side. The men stabbed with swords or fired flintlocks at the monster—*at the kraken*?

Even though his men fought fiercely, long thorn-crusted limbs continued to pulverize the ship. Several sailors writhed on the deck, blood oozing from their wounds. One lay still.

Fear swelled inside Modo's chest, but determination drowned all his insecurities. Captain Modo unsheathed a sword and threw himself into the fray.

He made quick work of slicing through the nearest limb. The dismembered piece wriggled aimlessly until a wave crested the ship's damaged side. Sea water mingled with the kraken's dark blood, and a man beside him slipped. The severed tentacle knocked the sailor down. Sweat clouded Modo's vision, but he grabbed the man, then attacked the kraken with all his strength.

Sailors struggled to keep their feet in the carnage, but despite its injuries, the kraken continued to toss the ship. Modo's muscles burned with exertion. His head still pounded, but exhaustion could not make him waver.

His crew's strength was fading, but the monster's attack had slowed, when Bella appeared in Modo's peripheral vision. She swung a sword using the moves Quinn taught her. The blade was much too heavy and her movements were sluggish and awkward. A horrible flash of nightmare—Bella kidnapped by the witch—seared through him.

"Bella, you should be in your cabin!" Modo yelled over the cacophony of clanging swords, curses, and kraken screeches.

"No, I should not!"

Modo barely dodged a tentacle. "Don't argue. Go!"

Bella sideswiped another limb. "You're not my commander."

"I'm the captain of this ship! I'm everyone's commander."

Clearly, the kraken had come specifically for her as the monster loosened its hold around the *Notre Dame*, and wrapped its remaining tentacles around her small frame. Bella lost her grip. Her sword clanked onto the deck. The beast sank into the ocean.

Bella's choked shrieks stopped as the beast dragged her under. Modo screamed out her name, but it was too late. The ship stopped rocking. The only sound was that of the remaining crew's gasps for air. A hurricane of emotion replaced logic, and he raced to the side and dove into the sea after Bella.

Water closed in around him, the depths muffling his crew's shouts. His eyes adjusted to the sun-illuminated watery blues and teals of his surroundings. He swam in the direction the monster had taken Bella. Sword in hand Modo slashed at tentacles that crashed into him, but the ocean slowed his movements. His efforts had no effect.

The oxygen in his lungs disappeared. His insides felt like they were on fire, so Modo kicked until he reached the surface. He choked and sputtered between gulps of air. Every muscle in his body ached, yet the excruciating pain was in his heart. The one woman he loved had been taken away in an instant.

A rope splashed into the water only feet away, and he managed to hang on as his men pulled him onto the ship.

Jeb wrapped a jacket around Modo. The sun kept the water tepid, but Captain Modo shook as if it had been freezing.

Aerrol kneeled to look at Modo. "Captain, are you okay?"

"Wha' about Beller?" Jeb inquired.

"I couldn't—" Modo coughed. "I couldn't find her."

Tears welled up in Jeb's eyes. "Do ya finks she's dead?"

A lump formed in Modo's throat, and he swallowed hard.

Aerrol reached out a hand to assist the captain to his feet. There was no sign of the beast in the water and Modo's despair deepened.

"What was a kraken doing in these parts of the world?" Gregory asked. "I thought they were found off the coast of Norway."

Modo took a bracing breath. "We're in a world controlled by fae. Nothing will be typical on this journey." Jeb handed him his sword, already cleaned, and Modo sheathed it while he turned to face his somber crew. "I will not give up on Bella. She was entrusted into my care. My only mission was to get her home safely, and I will."

Jeb cheered, but Aerrol and Gregory exchanged looks. Most of the men regarded him with unreadable expressions.

"Cap'n," Jeb said, "where do we go now?"

Modo nodded at the red-haired man, then raised his voice to address everyone. "First, we need to finish cleaning up this mess. Then we can assess the damage, repair what we can, and inventory supplies to see what, if any, were lost. Lieutenant Flyntock, when that is finished, report back to me with a summary. I'll be in my quarters looking for a map and a method to track mythical sea creatures."

"Aye, aye, Captain," the men called out almost in unison.

The crew set to work, shoving the remaining tentacles into the sea and picking through the wreckage. Despite his fatigue, Modo made his way to the bow. His jaw clenched. Breaking down in anguish wasn't what a leader did. It wouldn't help him search for Bella if despair conquered determination.

He would succeed at rescuing Bella even if it killed him.

Before Modo headed to his own cabin, he stopped by Bella's. Her rose scent lingered in the room, and his anguish heightened. A cup of tea had been knocked to the floor near her chair, but while he watched, the cup and saucer mysteriously moved upright and placed themselves onto the table, proving Bella's claim the room was magicked with more than books. Modo paused. If there was a spell, there was a chance that the one who had made it was nearby.

"Aerowyn?" Modo called, but there was no answer.

Modo moved to sit in the comfy chair near the bookshelf.

For once, he wanted the enchantress to make an appearance. How was he going to rescue Bella if a mythical kraken stole her away? He wasn't convinced the beast was as it appeared, or it wouldn't have left the *Notre Dame* alone after taking Bella. It must have been sent to kidnap her, and no matter what Jeb said, that meant she was probably alive.

Did one of her books tell of where krakens lived?

Unbidden, other questions surfaced: Did all these tales have happy endings? Did some heroes never get their chance to rescue the people they loved?

His heart ached at the thought.

He ran his fingers through his disordered hair. Even in a world where the fae cast spells, he couldn't defeat an oversized squid. His dashing good looks wouldn't win him any battles, but his deformed hunched body wouldn't have been able to kill monsters. If he could have a second chance, maybe this body would be useful after all.

Modo was about to turn toward the door when the sound of water captured his attention. He turned. A soft rose scent emanated from the white bathtub, which was slowly filling with steaming water.

"Impossible," he whispered.

No pipe gushed water. He couldn't find the source, but a seashell floated to the surface. He blinked. Seashells didn't float. Modo grabbed it and turned it over to study it. On the other side, scrawled in neat handwriting, were three words:

*Callista has Bella.*

Fear-induced vigor replaced weariness, and he bolted to the upper deck. Both lieutenants were near the stairs, and he grabbed Gregory by the arm.

"Callista has Bella. If you—or anyone—has any idea how to find or defeat her, let me know. I'll be searching Bella's books for answers."

Aerrol raised a brow. "Callista? The sea witch who almost wrecked both the *Notre Dame* and the *Black Fear* with her tempest?

"Yes," Modo growled.

"Sir..." Gregory rubbed the back of his neck. "Why do you think that?"

"Because of this." Modo shoved the seashell into the lieutenant's hand. "It proves I am right about Bella being alive. But it also means I—we—need extra help to find her."

The taller lieutenant whistled. "Where did you get this?"

"Floating in Bella's bathtub." Sudden embarrassment at having been in Bella's quarters made heat rush to his face.

"Bella's tub?" Gregory asked. "What were you doing in—"

"The question is," Aerrol interrupted, "can we really trust something that appears in the middle of a tub full of water?"

"No, we can't." Gregory narrowed his eyes at the shell. "Could something be purposefully misleading us?"

Modo groaned. "I know that magic isn't always trustworthy, but I cannot—I *will not*—accept that she is dead."

His lieutenants looked at each other as if they were communicating without speaking. A shiver traveled down Modo's neck. They *knew*. He could see it on their faces. That the shell could even be treacherous, but they knew exactly what it meant.

"So," Gregory said, "what do we do?"

Modo scrubbed his hand over his face. "I don't know, except the answer has to be in Bella's library."

Aerrol studied him, then gave a short nod. "Then we'll keep an eye on things here."

Captain Modo strode back to Bella's quarters. Either the witch or one of her allies had sent that message. No matter where it had come from, he *would* find Bella if he had to read every blasted book on those shelves.

# Chapter 15

# Bellarose

B ella woke to the stench of mold and brine and the sound of water slapping against rock. For another moment, she lay on her back, then painstakingly sat up. Bella's teeth were chattering and she shivered uncontrollably. Even when she clutched her knees to her chest, the damp stone underneath chilled her. Everything hurt. Darkness worse than any moonless night hid everything, even when she waved her hand in front of her eyes.

With every sense on edge, Bella called out, "Is anyone here?"

Other than the lapping waves and echoes of her voice, all was silent. Maybe she was in a cave? Near the ocean—or *under* it? Was that even possible? She shuddered. Whether or not she was, she had no desire to jump into the cold water and explore when she was chilled to the bone. She probably wouldn't survive long enough to reach the surface anyway, so she rubbed her palms against her arms in an attempt to generate some body heat. Had she survived being dragged through the sea by a mythical creature, only to freeze to death instead?

"Please," Bella croaked. "Someone? Can anyone hear me?"

Should she move past her current spot when she couldn't see a thing? In this dark, damp place, was there anywhere warm? Anywhere safe? How far would she have to swim underwater? She couldn't allow this to be her end.

"Where am I? Is anyone out there?" She squeezed the words out through her pain.

A quiet cackle sent a shiver down her spine. That sound haunted her nightmares. Callista—the witch who had attempted to kill Cerise and everyone on the *Black Fear*—was in the cave.

"No one can hear you." The low, hoarse voice was exactly what Bella expected.

"Callista?"

"What gave me away?"

"Your laugh."

"When would you have heard me laugh before now? Wait... I remember. You were in that glorious typhoon I created to ruin King Peter's plan."

"Do you know what Peter and his daughter, Aerowyn have planned for me or the future?"

"No, but anything they are involved in, I try to foil."

Bella didn't ask why, but somewhere in her memory snippets of conversations with Aerowyn, under a different name, trickled through her mind. Were those talks, night visions, or something she was forced to forget? She shook her head. Now wasn't the time to decipher dreams.

"Is that why you brought me to your lair?"

"Technically, I didn't bring you here. My pet kraken did, but yes, I had him fetch you for me." The sound of the witch's heavy breathing echoed in the cave. "Peter is protecting you for some unfathomable reason. I brought you here to figure out why. I needed to be sure neither he nor his self-righteous daughter were on board so I could steal you away. If I can't solve the mystery, you will be added to my collection of slaves."

Hot, fishy smelling air crossed Bella's neck. She jumped, and bumps formed on her arms.

"You're so skittish, dearie. Can't you see in the dark?"

"No." Bella's voice quivered.

Callista whispered something in an unfamiliar language. The sound of wet skin pulled across a hard surface whispered through the cave, too soft to echo.

"Who else is in here?"

"You'll see soon enough." The sea witch chuckled harshly. "That was a pun. I sent my assistant to get something to light up the cave for your human eyes."

Bella raised her chin in false bravado. "I doubt Peter knows you took me. His plans can't be ruined if he isn't even aware I was kidnapped."

Callista cackled again. "You're funny. He knows. Believe me, he and his sanctimonious daughter, Aerowyn know. They think they're so superior, but it is *his* fault I look the way I do." Almost tangible bitterness oozed out of her voice.

The odd *schlsh schlsh* cut through the darkness. A green glow emanated from the mossy plant in Callista's minion's hand. Its faint illumination was bright enough to show Bella the terrifying images of both Callista and the partial man.

In full form, Callista wasn't exactly a mermaid or a woman. She had a woman's upper body with arms and a sea shell pendant attached to a hemp chain around her neck. Her lower tubular body was similar to a gigantic eel with a sickly chartreuse skin. On her head was a tuft of seaweed-like hair. Her smooth, glossy tail writhed as she smirked down at Bella.

Callista's underling was male, and his black hair matched his slick coal-black eel-like skin. Both bodies unnerved Bella, but when she met the underling's eyes, she gasped.

"J-jasper, is that you?"

Familiar blue eyes stared into hers from the transformed face. The shape was the same—but the color... His whole body was now as jet-black as his slick hair. Jasper's eyes hadn't changed, except for the fear that shone even in this pale light. The confident, handsome rogue of a pirate who had stolen her from New Orleans was hideous.

"He can't answer you." Callista gloated. Her scratchy voice grated on Bella's nerves. "I temporarily took his tongue."

"But he transformed into a magnificent merman for Cerise. How is he stuck—" Bella caught herself before finishing the sentence with, *serving a sea hag's wishes.* Antagonizing Callista would help neither of them, but the sight made her shivers worse.

She chattered. "What d-d-did you d-d-do t-to him?"

"It's only a temporary spell to persuade his mermaid to obey my wishes. Cerise is going to make sure that fiend, Peter, gets my message in case he didn't notice when my pet brought you here." Callista crossed her human arms over her eel chest. "You, however, are my prisoner until King Peter gives me back my glorious body."

Bella groaned. She couldn't survive the cave's frigid temperatures, and her shivering made every bruise and scratch the kraken had inflicted hurt even more.

Callista studied her like a science specimen. "Your rattling teeth are giving me a headache. Use your supernatural abilities and get warm."

Bella's shivering made speaking difficult. "I d-don't have any. I'm j-j-ust a g-g-girl."

The sea witch clicked her tongue. "I don't understand. You don't have magic. You're not strong. You're not even that pretty. Why in Triton's beard would Peter need you?"

The cold began to disappear, and Bella could barely keep her eyes open. The insults didn't even sting anymore.

"She can't die yet. I need her as a bargaining tool," Callista screeched. "Do something!"

Clammy skin touched Bella's flesh as strong arms enveloped her. She knew that grip. It had only been one-handed before, and the familiar touch was not comforting. Jasper's body was like marble and did nothing to warm her, even when he rubbed cold hands up and down her arms.

A muzzy sensation crept through Bella's mind, and the shivering stopped.

Callista smacked her lips. "I guess we're going to have to move her to a better climate, but where?"

Numbing iciness dragged Bella into unconsciousness, pushing her toward eternity.

# Chapter 16

# Gerard

Lieutenants Aerrol Flyntock and Gregory Butler waited for Captain Modo to leave before they found a place away from listening ears to discuss recent events. Mental communication was more difficult when Gregory was double hexed. Being a man turned to wolf then turned into a different man taxed his body and mind.

Gregory cursed and looked straight into Aerrol's eyes. "Aerowyn, what did you allow happen?"

"Shhh!" Aerrol hissed. "Speak quietly. When I look like Aerrol, you must address me that way."

"I already checked. No one is within ear-shot." Gregory scanned the room again. "Why did you allow Bella to be kidnapped?"

"I didn't." Aerrol scowled at Gregory and whispered harshly, "I don't have control over Callista. She has her own magic. Also, I can't keep track of where that witch is at all times."

Gregory puffed out. "You could have stopped the kraken with your spells, or better yet, you could have killed it."

Aerrol motioned Gregory to follow, and they moved to the cargo hold.

"Please keep your volume down!" Aerrol whispered sternly. "I didn't want to kill the beast, and my magic had no control over it. I tried while everyone was distracted by its attacks."

Gregory's fury simmered while he pondered her confession.

"What do you mean you had no control over the kraken?"

"I didn't understand it at first, but once Modo showed us that seashell, I knew why I couldn't stop the kraken. I noticed it in battle with Callista during the storm. Worry lines stretched across Aerrol's forehead and he added, "She seems to be getting stronger."

Gregory's stomach churned as he considered the consequences. Aerowyn hadn't explained everything to him before they joined Modo's crew, but sometimes she let ideas flow to him about the importance of Bella's happy ending. Did he dare ask her now or were there more pressing things to consider?

"I know you want to ask me something. Go ahead," Aerrol said.

Gregory frowned. "If you know, then why don't you answer the question."

"I think I know the reason I have less control over Callista's powers, but we need to go back to Ageless Isle before—"

Shoes clomped down the stairs, and Aerrol stopped talking. They hid behind barrels of gun powder to avoid being seen.

The sailor began counting out loud, "One, two..."

He must have been sent down to inventory the supplies and inspect any damage the kraken could have done.

Aerrol huffed. "We don't have time for this. Father needs us home now."

The golden scepter appeared and spun around Aerrol. Instantly Aerowyn, with her long sparkling golden hair and brown eyes replaced Lieutenant Aerrol Flyntock.

Gregory pressed his palms together and pleaded, "Must I go back to being a wolf? It's been heartening to have human conversations and to not be knee-level all the time."

The crewman stepped into the hold. When he saw Aerowyn and Gregory, he gasped. "Blimey! What are you doing on our ship?"

Aerowyn waved the wand and whispered, "You will forget you saw us and go to the crow's nest to look for mermaids."

The sailor's face went blank, and he left Aerowyn and Gregory alone.

Aerowyn frowned at Gregory sympathetically. "Now back to the task at hand. I told you that being Gregory Butler was temporary." She spoke tenderly. "You'll return to your normal body after the curse is broken. This glamor won't stick." She reminded Gregory. "I was hoping to keep our disguises longer, but this short-term spell can't hold against the wolf curse. Besides, now that Bella has been kidnapped again—"

"I know. Our reasons for being lieutenants are null." He lowered his head dejectedly.

Gregory winced, and moans accompanied each motion. His vision blurred temporarily, and sounds of torn clothing replaced whimpers. As Gregory morphed into a wolf his eyesight became keener. Thick black fur covered what used to be his arms, and he panted heavily. Aerowyn crouched beside him and caressed his fur. Gerard leaned into her. She lifted his chin and peered into his eyes. He barked quietly and licked her hands in wordless communication.

Aerowyn's lips pursed. She touched Gerard's fur and his skin tingled. His sensitive nose detected the scent of magic while his muscles tensed knowing he was about to feel the weightlessness of moving through space too rapidly. He watched Aerowyn's skirts turn invisible while they evaporated into mist on their way back to Ageless Isle.

# Chapter 17

# Bellarose

B ella awoke in unfamiliar surroundings again. A bamboo frame woven with greenery fluttered overhead, and a bed of palm leaves crinkled underneath her. The scents of tropical flowers and vegetation wafted into her shelter. In the distance, waves lapped gently over sand. She was much warmer, but she had no idea if eels could live out of water for long. Maybe, Callista had forced someone—or something—to keep Bella as a prisoner on land. Bella propped herself up on her elbows.

"You're awake!"

Bella turned her body toward the sophisticated feminine voice. A large iridescent dragon glared down at her. Bella's heart beat in her chest like a trapped humming bird.

"Don't be afraid." The soprano timbre and delicate English accent didn't match the mammoth body. "I promised Callista, I wouldn't harm you even though I love the taste of roasted human."

"Who are you?" Bella licked her lips and scooted farther from the reptile, whose genteel voice didn't fool her for a second. "And where am I?"

"I'm Eira, another victim of King Peter's tyranny. You're on an island near Ageless Isle." The dragon leaned down to eye level. "But don't think that because you're close to Peter's home that he will rescue you."

"I won't." Bella's voice trembled.

Eira was another perfect example of King Peter's misplaced attempt to rid the world of selfishness and cruelty. Her scheme for revenge was terrifying.

Bella's voice quaked. "How did I get here?"

"Callista and her slimy eel minion dropped you off on the shore, and since neither of them can be out of water for very long, she summoned me. I get to be the human-sitter." She huffed—a frightening thing in a dragon. "From what I hear, Callista's cave is foul so you're better off with me anyway. This isn't my home, either, but at least we're far from prying busy-bodies."

Bella darted her eyes over her surroundings before focusing on the winged creature again. "Is this island deserted?"

"No." Eira's mouth turned upward. "In fact, I threatened some of the locals that I would roast them for dinner if they didn't make this little shelter and bed for you. For obvious reasons." The dragon displayed her clawed talons. "Since I can't build anything."

The reptile shifted, and behind her several trees had been flattened.

"If this island isn't your home, do you come from Terradraco?"

Eira narrowed her eyes at Bella. "How do you know about that place?"

Bella pulled her shaking arms into her sides to steady them. "It's the setting of my favorite fairy tale, *The Scorned Fae,* which I was told was a true story. It's the only place I've ever heard of dragons living."

Eira puffed out another breath and Bella ducked in fear of flames. The beast shifted while she stared at Bella. "That dragon-infested place is only my home since I became one."

Bella tried to peer past the gigantic beast, but Eira was too large. Even so, a distant part of Bella's mind acknowledged that she was handling the confrontation well. A year ago, she wouldn't have believed any of this–kraken, sea witch, or dragon—but now she at least knew she wasn't hallucinating.

"Anyway, thank you for this shelter." Bella forced her voice to steady. "But why am I here?"

"I don't know all the details, but if it means I can return to my former self, I'm willing to do anything—and I mean anything."

Silver irises with black-slit pupils stared at Bella menacingly. Acid rose in Bella's throat as images of becoming a dragon's skewered dinner over a self-made flame popped into her mind. Freezing to death in a cave was preferable to being flame broiled by a dragon with a penchant for human flesh.

She moved farther from the beast, and Eira laughed like a proper noble lady. The small dainty titter was shocking, coming from such a large animal.

"My dear girl, I'm not going to eat you." Eira snickered again. "I like to tease, and evidently you took me seriously. I may be a creature who craves meat, but I've never eaten a human and don't intend on trying one anytime soon. I was human once, and I'm not a cannibal. I will go hungry before considering a roasted man-leg as a side dish." Eira gagged. "Great Jehoshaphat, I just vomited in my mouth at the thought of chomping down on a hairy sinewy male leg."

Bella's stomach turned, too, at the thought of Eira feasting on human flesh as if it were a turkey leg, but the dragon's unusual reaction made Bella curious.

Having heard enough discussion of eating people, Bella asked, "How will keeping me a prisoner help you or Callista? I'm only a girl with no magical skills. I tried to explain that to Callista, but she wouldn't listen."

"If Peter and his daughter think you're valuable, he will do anything to keep you safe. That is what we're counting on."

What on earth did Peter and Aerowyn want from her? And would Peter be able to reverse his curses to keep her safe? Would he want to?

Before she could ask more, Bella's stomach growled.

Eira chortled. "My, my, that was loud. I suppose you haven't eaten for a long time. I can catch you a rabbit and cook it for you. What do you want?"

Bella hesitated. The idea of a dragon bringing her food was disconcerting.

"Has the cat got your tongue? It doesn't have to be rabbit. I've been in this form for so long that I have forgotten what I liked to feast upon when I was human, although I remember lavish parties at the palace and delectable sweets." She tapped a massive claw on the sand. "I can't give you cake, if that's what you're craving."

"I don't want anything like that. A rabbit will do. Are berries nearby, or something I could forage for myself?"

Eira growled. "You aren't allowed to explore. I must keep an eye on you so you don't escape or get rescued, as improbable as *that* is." She added smugly, "I'm actually the only thing the fae are afraid to mess with, which makes me a perfect warden."

Bella studied the dragon. While she wasn't lovely in the traditional sense, she had an exotic beauty. Bella was surprised by her admiration of Eira's prism-like scales and shiny silver eyes. She normally thought reptiles were ugly, but this dragon's appearance was alluring.

She drew a breath and asked, "So it's true what I read in *The Scorned Fae*? A dragon's fire is the only thing to kill immortals?"

"Don't believe everything you read in books. Dragon fire may have seemed to have fixed the problem, but it was only temporary."

"What do you mean?"

"*The Scorned Fae* was that book about Isla, Peter's other daughter who defied him and turned a human into a dragon because the man wouldn't marry her."

Curiosity replaced Bella's hunger. "Yes, I remember. But what do you mean that was only a temporary fix? A fix for what problem?"

"It's in your perspective. Which character's crisis was being repaired?"

"Why not tell me all perspectives," Bella suggested, "and let me have my own opinion?"

Eira's mouth curled up, but rather than menacing, her expression mimicked a dainty duchess.

The bizarre contrast of the monstrous dragon being coquettish reminded Bella of the fantastical animals in that strange book in her library, *Alice in Wonderland*.

"Well, that makes you unique," the dragon said. "Your desire to hear a story is greater than your need to eat. I'll get you a rabbit, then tell you what you want to know. There will be plenty of time for history lessons. Come out from that shelter."

Bella obeyed, and Eira rose onto her hindlegs and grabbed a large cage made of bones, which she plopped over Bella. Sand flew and stung Bella's skin as the dragon took off. Once Bella was alone, she tried to lift the contraption to escape, but it was too heavy. Bella backed to the center, scrubbing her hands over her dress. Eira herself could not have fashioned the cage, but perhaps she had intimidated the local people to fabricate the trap as well.

*I hope these aren't human bones.*

It wasn't long before Eira was back with the roasted rabbit. She lifted the cage and dropped the carcass in front of Bella. The smell of its charred fur made Bella dry heave.

"Oh dear, what is happening to you?" Eira asked.

"I'm not accustomed to eating meat with fur and head still intact. It's—" before she could finish explaining she gagged again.

Without even replacing the bone cage, Eira snatched away the singed carcass and flew off. She returned before Bella had recovered. In her left talons, she carried a young woman about Bella's age, and in her right, she held the dead rabbit.

Eyes downcast, the resigned young woman stood by the dragon's claws and made no attempt to run away. Her dingy gray, threadbare shirt was similar to the style Jasper used to wear. The men's britches tied around her waist could have belonged to a pirate captain, but they were too big for the girl's slender frame. The only new thing she wore was an apron woven from palm fronds, and the only bright color was her hair, an unusual pink hue that swung in a thick braid.

Eira seemed pleased with herself.

"This girl built your temporary shelter. She has a knife and the ability to skin the rabbit to make it more appealing to your senses."

Bella wiped her hands onto her skirt and managed, "What is your name? I'm Bella."

"She can't talk. Callista took her tongue—she's always doing things like that. This young lady used to be a mermaid, but now she lives on this island with all the other merfolk who infuriated the sea hag." The dragon spewed out a flame. "Oops, did I say that out loud? Don't let Callista know." She grew serious. "And never let her hear your true opinion because she's rather temperamental. Probably half of the island's population is merfolk who criticized her over something trivial. I may be a dragon, but I still follow some rational thinking before scorching my enemies."

Bella didn't know whether to cringe or giggle at the dragon's outlandish comments.

Instead, she smiled at the mermaid and then turned to Eira. "Even though she can't talk, am I allowed to speak to her? What is her name?"

"If you don't mind having a one-sided conversation, then by all means talk until your own tongue falls out." The dragon shrugged one colossal shoulder. "I don't know her name. When I want her attention, I point to her and make my demands. Is it important?"

"Of course it's important," Bella said softly, but she didn't explain.

After the past few months of being kidnapped and losing her autonomy, Bella understood how difficult it was to have her choices taken away, and her heart went out to the young woman.

The mermaid smiled slightly at Bella.

"Fine, then. I'll call her Pinky." When the girl grimaced, the dragon snorted. "Because of her hair."

The young woman occasionally glanced at Bella as she pulled the skin off the rabbit. The meat wasn't cooked all the way, so the mermaid built a fire and made quick work of roasting the flesh on a stick. When the rabbit was done, she handed the food to Bella.

"Thank you. Do you want some?"

The girl shook her head, her aqua-colored eyes darting between Bella and the dragon, but she kept her head bent mostly as if cowering in fear.

Eira laughed. "She doesn't eat land animals, you ignorant girl. She came from the ocean. Probably likes fish or seaweed."

"I'm sorry. I didn't think. I appreciate you helping me. I would have done that myself, but I suppose they don't want me to have a knife."

"No weapons for prisoners, even if I did make an exception with Pinky here. I promised her that if she helps me with your needs that I'll put in a good word with Callista. Perhaps the harpy will show mercy and give her back her tongue and tail."

Once it had cooled enough to touch, Bella peeled the meat off the bones. It wasn't as good as meals Finn prepared aboard the *Notre Dame*, but as long as she was a prisoner, she'd take what she could get.

Eira put the bone cage back over Bella before she had finished eating and lifted the speechless mermaid by her apron. Loneliness engulfed Bella like never before. Even after her parents died, there was always another person she could talk to. Maybe they weren't always friendly conversations, but they had kept the isolation away. Now the silence was deafening. The typical sounds of the jungle with animals scurrying and bugs clicking their wings couldn't replace the dissonance of utter separation from humanity.

# Chapter 18

# Captain Modo

After the fight with the kraken, the crew immediately began repairs aboard the *Notre Dame*. The ship had been forced off course and was sailing between uncharted floating islands. Modo wasted no time searching for clues among Bella's books.

The sound of hammering and scent of citrus and spice from the islands filled the air. Modo glanced out of Bella's cabin window at the azure ocean. The water's mystical appearance and the balmy temperature would have comforted Modo's nerves if he wasn't thinking of the likely proximity to Ageless Isle. The clusters of land masses he had spotted upon the poop deck should have only existed in fairy tales.

Magic was a mystery to him, but Bella's kidnapping had placed her in the center of this whole mess. She read voraciously. Surely Aerowyn had left information in at least one book.

Modo tried to concentrate as he ran his fingers over the books' spines, searching for a title that might hold a clue. It didn't make sense that Callista wanted Bella. She was only a girl without any enchantment skills. Aerowyn must have ties to the whole situation, but he had no way to contact her to ask. She didn't give him a signal to use in case he needed her and screaming into the night sky would only make him look like he'd lost his sanity. Instead, he mumbled the titles hoping they would bring him closer to finding the girl he loved.

"*The Scorned Fae, The King's Curse, Pirates and Mermaids, Beauty and the Wolf.*"

They sounded like Bella's adventures. She mentioned *The Scorned Fae* was one of her favorites. He had taken it at the beginning of the journey, but returned it before Bella missed it. He pulled the thin volume from the shelf and opened it.

The adventure of a prince turning into a dragon, only to be changed back to his real form by true love's kiss sounded fanciful... Except that Modo had been transformed from, in his opinion, a hideous creature. In fact, Gerard and Jasper were altered too. Modo massaged his temple.

"Could the story be real?" He paced as he addressed the empty room. "Is this Isla somehow related to Aerowyn? Are these the fae that have been magicking people into other creatures?"

"Cap'n!"

Modo startled and dropped the book as Jeb bounded into Bella's quarters like a bull in a china shop.

"What is it Jeb?'

"Gilbert spotted—mer—crow's nest—" Jeb heaved in and out breaths with incoherent speech.

Modo didn't wait for the explanation and sprinted to the upper deck where all the crew was looking beyond the bow. There bobbing above the water was Cerise's fire-colored hair.

Her melodic voice shouted, "Captain Modo, I need to talk to you."

The sun began to dip toward the horizon turning the aqua hues of the ocean to darker blues. The gentle breeze carried a light scent of brine.

"I'm here." Modo bellowed over the sound of water lapping the ship's sides.

Worry and angst was evident on Cerise's face. "Callista has Bella. She is using me as a messenger."

"Are you the one who left the shell message?"

"Yes. I was hoping that Aerowyn was aboard your ship. Callista wants to barter with Aerowyn or her father, Peter for Bella's freedom." She sobbed out, "Callista has Jasper too." The tide forced the water over her head, and she dipped below the surface, remerging to sputter, "Callista cursed Jasper with a body like her own and forced me to be her messenger, or she will kill him."

"Why don't you join us on deck," Modo asked, "so we don't have to keep yelling?"

"I can't—" Water submerged her. She popped her head up again. "Aerowyn's spell."

"Don' ya 'member Cap'n?" Jeb whispered.

"That's right. The only way she could live after Callista had stabbed her was to share a heart with Jasper, but the price for the magic meant they had to remain in the ocean forever." Modo shifted uncomfortably. Jasper's touching sacrifice of giving up half his heart had been a warning that all magic had a price.

"Cerise," Modo yelled. "We don't know how to reach Aerowyn, but could you lead us to Bella?"

Cerise's head went under the water and then she yelled, "Yes, follow me."

Modo put his palm up in the air. "Wait! Can our ship follow you where you're going?"

She stopped swimming and shook her head.

Jeb squared his shoulders. "I'll take our skiff ou' there and talk wif her."

Modo nodded. "That would be best. Tell her we'll help rescue Jasper or try to find Aerowyn, but we think Bella is in more imminent danger."

The crew lowered the smaller rowing boat with Jeb in it so that he could be closer to Cerise. The sun dipped below the horizon, and they lit the lanterns. After Jeb and the mermaid finished talking, the crew hoisted Jeb back onto the ship.

"What did she say?" Modo demanded.

Jeb frowned. "Beller is a dragon's prison'r."

Curses and gasps echoed among the crew. Skeptical expressions washed over some, but most seemed resigned to both magic and myth after fighting the kraken. The captain stood on the elevated quarter deck, and a small breeze tossed Modo's hair as he projected his voice for all to hear, even Cerise.

"Men, I pledged to transport Bella safely to Louisiana." Modo lifted his chin with conviction. "I must rescue her. I will not force any of you to come with me. Jeb has told us we will face a dragon. We have faced a kraken, so I know you are brave, but I have no idea what other monsters await." Modo swallowed to stop the quiver in his voice, hoping no one would see his fear. "Given this new information about Bella's captor, I shall not think less of you should you choose to stay on the ship. We may return maimed. We may lose our lives. If you're willing to take the risk for Bella, then follow me to the jolly boat."

He moved from the quarter deck to board the skiff.

Jeb, of course, was the first to step forward. While the kraken had injured many, almost all who could walk followed Jeb. A knot formed in Modo's throat seeing how the crew loved her, too.

Modo looked around. "Where are Lieutenant Butler and Flyntock? I want to put them in charge while I'm absent."

Gilbert, who had exited the crow's nest after he sighted Cerise stepped forward. "Captain, I saw something strange happen between the lieutenants, but as soon as I questioned them, I got all muddled. It's coming back to me now, but you're not going to believe me." The man squirmed.

Modo drew in a heavy breath. "Tell me, and I'll be the judge of what I will believe."

"Well... um... Lieutenant Flyntock turned into the most beautiful woman I've ever seen."

Some who heard his confession chuckled and others let out whistles.

A former pirate whispered, "He's been drinking too much grog."

Another sailor asked, "Did he say he saw a woman on our ship besides Bella?"

"Silence!" Modo looked at Gilbert. "Did she have a gold scepter?"

"Yes, but how did you know?"

Modo exhaled. "It was probably Aerowyn, the enchantress."

"No sir. I saw the enchantress when we were in the storm and wait—" Gilbert scratched his beard and then finished, "I guess she looked similar to Aerowyn."

Modo straightened his waistcoat. "She can take on the appearance of anyone. She fooled us all, and I would bet a year's wages, Lieutenant Butler was her wolf."

Gilbert shrugged his shoulders. "I don't know Captain. It's like I said, she cast some haze over me and told me to go look for mermaids in the crow's nest. I was compelled to obey and then I spotted Cerise."

Modo scanned the crowd. "Quartermaster, Westley."

"Aye, aye, Captain." A young blond-haired man approached Modo and saluted.

"Men, obey Westley's orders in my absence." Modo addressed those staying and then turned to the volunteers. "All right men, be brave and steadfast. Bella needs us."

The skiff wasn't large, so only Modo and the first five men could go. The rest of the volunteers solemnly handed over knives, swords, and loaded muskets. The men crowded the ship's railing while two sailors lowered the jolly boat. The mermaid surfaced as the boat hit the water, rocking slightly when the men picked up the oars. Cerise swam ahead, leading them to a smaller isle located to the west.

As they grew closer, Cerise angled to the island's southern shore and slowed so she could speak softly. "The island is so small that you can walk around it in one hour. Eira is keeping Bella on the north side, and she'd most likely spy anyone approaching from that direction. Callista's underwater cave, where Bella was originally kept prisoner, isn't too far from Eira's camp. It's deeper down, which means the witch might see me and your watercraft. Also, my people—the ones Callista cursed—live on the southern side of the isle. They'll help you sneak up on the dragon undetected."

The men reached the shore. Jeb and others jumped out and pulled the skiff through the shallow water to the sand.

"I wish you the best of luck in retrieving Bella." Cerise's voice carried over the lapping shore.

"Thank you." Modo bowed. "Will we ever see you again?"

"Probably." She nodded. "I wish you well, but I must try to rescue Jasper."

The mermaid dove completely under the sea. The men hoisted themselves out of the boat into the shallow water and pulled it ashore to a nearby palm tree. After tying the line around the palm so the skiff wouldn't float away, they silently trudged inland. Their ocean-soaked boots would take forever to dry in the island's moist and humid climate.

Exotic flowers, rich soil, and something unidentifiable scented the rich air. Sweat pooled on Modo's forehead and upper lip, and insects buzzed around him and occasionally stuck to his skin. The dense vegetation along with the crowded spaces of palm, coconut, and banana trees provided camouflage and shade. Modo and his crew progressed slowly through the jungle's natural obstacles.

He cleared his throat. "I think we should find the cursed merfolk first."

"I agree wif ya, sir." Jeb said.

Modo stifled a smile. Although Jeb was primarily the ship's tailor, he was as stalwart a crewmember as the quartermaster.

The sailors stuck close to Modo as they wended through the jungle, but as Cerise explained, the island was small. In about ten minutes, they found a quirky little village of bamboo and palm huts. People attired in odd clothing possibly salvaged from shipwrecks emerged, and a young woman whose vibrant pink hair identified her as a former mermaid approached them.

Modo inclined his head. "Good day, ma'am. I am Captain Modo of the *Notre Dame*."

She nodded back.

"Cerise said you would be able to assist us in rescuing Bella, the dragon's captive."

The young woman moved her hands in front of her mouth and then shook her head. She mouthed words but said nothing while she repeated the odd hand gestures.

"Me finks she can't talk, Cap'n," Jeb observed.

She nodded in affirmation and pointed to the others, whose strange hair and shelled adornments testified that they were the merfolk Cerise told Modo to find.

"Cap'n," Jeb said slowly, "I don't fink any of them can talk."

The mermaid nodded again.

"I can't imagine what that witch has done to you," Modo said, "but we need your help to save Miss Bonnay."

It would have been nice if Aerowyn returned these merfolks' speech as a reward for their aid, but since she wasn't there to make that promise, he hoped they would assist him even without that bribe.

The former merfolk gathered close, their heads all bobbing up and down to demonstrate their willingness to help. Several drew maps and pictures in the sand, and after questions and clarifications, everyone had an assigned task.

Modo could only trust they would be able to free Bella without risking anyone's life, but unforeseen things could alter all their careful plans.

He stepped back and crossed his arms. If this failed, he would try one more thing on his own.

# Chapter 19

# Gerard

Mental telepathy was both the best and worst skill Gerard had in wolf form.

*Why didn't we stay on the Notre Dame as the lieutenants?* he asked Aerowyn. *We could have helped Modo save Bella.*

"We needed to be here," she replied out loud. "Father told me to stay on Ageless Isle."

Even though Gerard was a wolf again, he was thankful for the change in scenery. He liked the feel of unmoving ground beneath his feet—or paws—and he felt steadier when the floor wasn't in constant movement.

Gerard's canine senses were extra stimulated from the scents only found on Ageless Isle. Even though Aerowyn had transported them directly into her home, and they hadn't walked through the forest like on his first visit, the scents of rich soil and strange vegetation penetrated the walls of Aerowyn's tree home.

He plopped down onto the dog bed in the corner of her living area, which connected to the kitchen and reminded Gerard of his quaint home in France where he spent most of his life. Aerowyn put a kettle on the stovetop. It was fueled by a special moss that burned continually without heating the house. Gerard's nostrils flared. She must be upset. She only prepared the strange smelling tea when she was stressed.

*Are you nervous?*

She frowned at him. "No. Why?"

Gerard sat up to look her in the eyes. *You told me once that you drank that tea for its calming abilities.*

Aerowyn fidgeted with her hair, then sighed. "I found out through mental communication with Cerise that Callista has entrusted Eira, a dragon, to keep Bella a prisoner."

*Is that why you won't help Modo? Are you afraid?* Gerard immediately regretted the question. Dragon fire would kill her, and he didn't want that.

Perpendicular lines formed between her brows. The kettle whistled and she turned to remove it from the flame and poured steaming water into her gold cup. She sat down at the table and sipped her tea. Gerard stood and nuzzled up against her, and with a sigh, she brushed her fingers through his fur.

Eventually, he broke the silence between them. *How is Bella supposed to fix the mess your father caused when she keeps being kidnapped?*

Aerowyn sipped more of her tea. "Father said Bella's happy ending would repair the fairy tales."

Gerard grumbled, *I know you've told me that before, but what does it mean?*

"Honestly, I wonder the same thing. Father says that Bella has a rare imagination, and if she finally gets her heart's desire, she'll fix everything, but he didn't tell me how. I doubt he even knows. It's as if he keeps grasping at solutions, and when one fails, he tries another one."

*I know you love him, but I'm glad you are no longer blind to his flaws.*

"I'm not." She lowered her voice. "I plan on leaving him and this world as soon as I finish my mission with Bella."

Panic tore through Gerard's furry chest. He didn't want to remain a wolf in a world without Aerowyn. He didn't want to be in any form without her. *You want to leave? But where would you go, and will I be able to accompany you?*

Her eyes deepened to the color of chocolate, and she tenderly whispered, "Are you asking to come along with me?"

*I would go with you anywhere. I have a confession to—*

"No, don't." She smiled tentatively. "If you're going to admit your true feelings to me, I want to hear them when you're a man." Aerowyn rubbed behind his ears and kissed the top of his head.

Gerard's tail thwacked loudly on the wooden floor to the beat of his ecstatic heart. Her actions told him she knew he was about to admit he loved her and the idea wasn't repulsive—in fact she was receptive to it.

*I hope I'm able to confess my feelings sooner rather than later. You know how quickly I told Elayne—the girl you pretended to be—how I felt after such a short time of knowing her. Back when I was a soldier and you were Elayne, I learned that war teaches life is short, and you may not have the chance to say the words tomorrow.*

"You forget," she said thickly. "We're immortal. We have forever."

*Forever can be shorter than you think. What if I'm taken away from you? What about when you leave?*

Aerowyn's eyes changed colors from brown to blue to violet, finally settling into a mixture of them all.

Gerard couldn't read her emotions when her eyes wouldn't settle on one tint. After all, when the hues transformed rapidly, she was confused or fighting with herself. He, however, knew exactly what his heart wanted.

His happily ever after could only be spent with Aerowyn.

# Chapter 20

# Bellarose

While Eira dozed, Bella etched one notch on her bone cage by using the sharp edge of a broken shell she found under her palm bed.

*Only two days. It seems like ten!*

She blew out a quiet breath. Bella's body ached from all the perils she had been through. Plus, every time a strange noise sounded from the jungle, her already sore muscles tensed. Even with the dragon protecting her from potentially dangerous creatures, her nerves were raw from worry, and her mind worked overtime, scheming for a way to escape. Could she convince Eira to work against Callista rather than for her?

At the sound of soft footsteps, Bella tucked the shell back in her pocket. The pink-haired girl nodded at her as she stepped into the glade, a bowl in her hands.

"I didn't ask you to come, Pinky." Eira raised her long white iridescent snout and glared at the girl. "What do you have there, anyway?"

"It looks like fruit," Bella said. "As much as I appreciate the meat you've provided, I'm craving fruit."

"Pshaw! I've never heard of something so ridiculous," the dragon scoffed. She narrowed her enormous eyes. "Although... Yes, I remember. When I lived in the palace, I loved sweets like fruit and pastries."

She puffed up her chest. "Now I have zero desire for anything but animal flesh."

The tailless mermaid handed Bella the dish through the bars of bones, tipping the large clam-shell bowl to fit it through the opening. It touched Bella's hands, and she tensed. Was that a piece of paper under the shell? She met the girl's eyes, and the former mermaid nodded, then padded toward a knocked over palm tree trunk to sit down. While Eira focused on the tongueless girl, Bella slipped the paper into her pocket to read later, when Eira left to fetch more meat.

Bella plunked down on the sand—her dress was already ruined, so there was no reason to be careful—and ate the peeled golden yellow chunks of pineapple. At first bite, juice dribbled down her chin and she sighed while using her sleeve to wipe off the mess. The sugary fruit taste was divine.

"Oh, thank you," she said to the young woman. "This is wonderful. Meat is better to stop the hollow feeling when your stomach is empty, but this feeds my sweet tooth." She hummed blissfully.

"I'm feeling a bit empty myself," Eira admitted. "I'll go hunting. Pinky, you stay here, then you can cook up another rabbit for the prisoner."

The girl scrunched up her face and nodded. Bella didn't think the former mermaid liked the name.

The unpredictable dragon swiveled her head to Bella. "Unless you prefer a monkey or something else?"

"No, rabbit is fine. I don't know how long I will be stuck here, but I can handle a few more days of rabbit or whatever bird you got me last time."

"That was a parrot."

Flashes of a childhood memory popped into her head. Again, the odd recollection seemed from a different era, but Bella dismissed that thought quickly. A friend owned a pet parrot that mimicked what people said. Bella's stomach knotted. Even though the animals on the isle were wild, she didn't want to eat someone's pet.

Eira's gigantic wings beat the air as she took off. After the beast had left, Bella hurriedly pulled the note out of her pocket.

*Dear Miss Bonnay,*

*We are on the island and plan on rescuing you with the aid of these hexed merfolk. All we need you to do is to convince Eira to let you out of the cage and distract her.*

*Sincerely,*

*Captain Modo*

Her insides flip-flopped again, but this time she smiled. Her expression sobered as she read the tidy handwritten instructions. She met the young woman's eyes, and they both nodded.

Rereading the short missive, she almost laughed at how formal it was. The memory of her impulsive kiss arose and she blushed. The fact that she had made a fool of herself would have to be temporarily forgotten. In order for the plan to work, she couldn't be distracted by her humiliation, and she couldn't afford to argue with someone who wasn't even here. How was she going to persuade Eira to allow her out of the cage and distract her with what? Unless... No, that was... well, embarrassing.

But now wasn't the time for stubborn independence.

The former mermaid tapped the cage and, when Bella looked up, pointed at the sky. Bella hastily shoved the note back into her pocket.

Eira dropped another dead rabbit in front of Bella.

"I already treated myself to a few wild boars, which I will share with you if I ever get full enough, but that should do for now."

"Yes, thank you." Bella drew a breath and did exactly what she needed to do.

"Eira, may I relieve myself before I eat?"

"Oh my, I forgot. Yes, I suppose using your cage would be a little off-putting for sleeping at night. Very well." The dragon lifted the cage partway, then paused. "I will kill Pinky if you try to escape. Modesty aside, you must return within a reasonable amount of time, or fried mermaid will be on the menu, and I'll never let you leave that cage again, bodily functions notwithstanding."

Bella avoided the mermaid's eyes and walked into the jungle where trees and bushes blocked her from Eira's view.

She hiked up her skirt, put her hand on her calf, counted to ten, then screamed.

"Snake! I've been bitten by a snake!"

Eira was there in a second, and Pinky followed.

"Was it poisonous?" The dragon sounded concerned. "Will it kill you?"

"I have no idea. I don't like snakes. I've never studied them. And what if it is some fae snake? It could have been a magical, dangerous species of reptile." Gasping, Bella doubled over like she was getting sick. "Uh, the world is spinning."

"Oh my, oh my, what to do, what to do?" Eira's voice hitched in panic.

Suddenly a group of sailors, merfolk, and Modo dropped from the trees with a net, noose, and rope. Jeb quickly tied the dragon's mouth; winding the rope multiple times around the jaw so she couldn't spew fire. The former merfolk holding the net wrapped it around Eira's body immobilizing her wings. In only a few seconds, she was on her side muzzled, bound, and tied to trees.

Panic and anger showed in Eira's eyes. Her pupils' black slits dilated, and she struggled against her bonds.

Captain Modo rushed to her side. "Bel—I mean Miss Bonnay, hurry. We don't know how long the ropes will hold."

Bella smiled up at him "I thought we were past formalities."

"Now is not the time to discuss how I address you. This is a rescue mission. Let's go."

"And I'm grateful, but—will she be hurt? Those ropes look very tight."

"I can't believe my ears." Modo sighed deeply. "Of course, you would worry for a dragon. She will eventually be able to escape her bonds. Hurry before she does."

Modo held his hand out for her to take, which shocked Bella into silent obedience.

Bella turned toward Eira. "I am sorry, but I have to go now. I trust you'll break free eventually."

The captain's hand in hers, they raced through the jungle until the undergrowth slowed them. When she stumbled, Modo lifted Bella up, and his strength gave her courage. She might have been running for her life, but she couldn't help seeing how robust and handsome the no-nonsense captain was.

Despite Modo's help, Bella's lungs burned for air. She wheezed and gasped, but his pace didn't allow her to breathe.

Modo halted, his deep brown eyes searching hers, "Are you well?"

"I-I-" Bella gasped. The world seemed dimmer. "I can-n't brea-"

Before she completed her sentence, Bella blacked out.

# Chapter 21

# Captain Modo

M odo scooped Bella into his arms and rushed to shore before the dragon could escape her temporary bindings. Bellarose was light and easy to carry, even in the sauna-like island's humidity.

He broke through the trees and reached the shore where his men and the merfolk were waiting.

"Blimey Cap'n, what took ya so long?" Jeb's eyes widened when he took in Bella. "What in Davey Jones's locker did you do to her?"

"Nothing!" Modo gritted his teeth. "Bella wasn't able to keep up with me and fainted."

Bella's eyes opened and she stammered, "Wha-a-t hap-pened?"

Modo spoke gently, "You fainted from the heat."

Her face bloomed red as Jeb helped load her into the crowded boat, and they rowed back to the ship, unloading Bella and most of the others. Then, Modo sent the skiff back to rescue every hexed mermaid and merman from the island before Eira broke free. After putting Westley, the quartermaster, in charge of the rescue with orders to set sail immediately afterward, he tended to Bella.

He handed her a scoop of fresh water, and she sat on a barrel to drink it.

"How are you feeling?"

Bella set the scoop down. "Exhausted and filthy." She examined her clothes. "I want to bathe and take a long nap."

"Do you need assistance returning to your quarters?" Modo tentatively placed his hand on her shoulder.

"No, I believe I can manage." She tilted her chin down and then whispered, "Thank you for rescuing me." Bella stood and brushed off the sand from her skirt. After she turned away from Modo, she took a few steps and looked back at him.

He smiled and tried to convey the unspoken message that all was fine between them. Her lips turned up in a tentative grin. She departed below deck, and Modo went to assist the quartermaster with the rest of the newcomers.

"Captain," Westley informed him, "the last group of merfolk are aboard."

Suddenly a tremendous splash rocked the boat. Callista shot out of the water and quickly grew into a larger-than-life yellow-green sea serpent.

Modo cursed silently as the hexed merman near him cowered in fear. At least Bella was as safe as she could be in her room—unless the ship splintered in half.

"All merfolk, get below," Modo shouted. "The rest of you, to arms!"

The rescued people raced and tumbled down to the hold as the crew sprinted up the ladders to the fighting mast and the cannons.

Modo turned to Westley. "How does one defeat a magical creature that big?" He tilted his head up to see the witch hit the mast.

The quartermaster grimaced and pulled out his flintlock pistol. "I don't know, sir, but we'll do our best."

"Man the cannons. I'll distract her."

Modo gave a curt nod, grabbed a sword, and ran to the poop deck. He jumped onto Callista, grunting as he landed and used the blade to hook himself onto her body, but she was too slippery. Modo lost his grip but managed to push the sword deeper into her thick skin. The witch didn't flinch. He reached down with his left hand and unsheathed the knife on his thigh. With brute strength, Modo stabbed Callista, and whether it was his blows or the cannon fire pummeling her side, she writhed.

Barely holding on, Modo knew Callista had to be destroyed before she hurt Bella. If Modo could climb up Callista's body and reach her eyes, he could blind her. He jerked the sword out, stabbed it again, hoisted himself up, but before he could strike again with the knife, Callista flung Modo into the sea.

Down, down, down—

Modo tossed the knife away and twisted feet first. He hit water hard as rock. The harsh azure swallowed him. He couldn't breathe. Flailing, he fought to climb to the surface, but which way was up?

He was going to die, and Bella wasn't going to have her perfect ending.

Then the roaring in his ears was silent, and all went black.

# Chapter 22

# Bellarose

Bella emerged from belowdecks to see Modo dangling from a pair of blades driven into a gigantic sea serpent's neck.

She cupped her hands around her mouth and shouted, "Hang on!"

But he was already plunging to the depths.

Bella clutched at her throat. From that distance, soft water would turn to an unforgiving surface. Modo could drown from his injuries. Bella kicked off her buckled shoes and, without pausing to think, jumped in after him.

Seconds after she hit the water, Bella realized her mistake. Her heavy skirt acted as an anchor. She quickly untied it and struggled to swim out of the weighted material. Although she knew how to swim, the turbulent water pulled at her. Every movement was a struggle. Straining her eyes, Bella peered through the depths and found the captain. His frantic movements stilled, and he began to sink. Without surfacing to take a breath, she swam down and grabbed his lifeless body. Her legs kicked laboriously against her petticoats. After what felt like hours, their heads broke through the ocean. Bella coughed and pounded on his back the best she could in the moving water, but he didn't wake.

"Where is the girl?" Callista's voice thundered.

Bella looked around. The crystal-clear water offered nowhere to hide.

"Bring her to me, and I will leave you all alone. I may even pull your drowning captain out of the depths before it's too late." Raucous laughter escaped her lips. "Never mind. I found her!"

Her serpentine body pivoted in the sea. With a triumphant screech, she scooped up Bella and Modo into her mouth. Her putrid breath made Bella's stomach churn.

Bella wrapped an arm around one of the creature's fangs and the other around the captain's chest, which moved shallowly. The serpent shot across the surface so quickly that ocean spray stung Bella's face. She clenched her eyes shut and tried not to breathe in the foul stench.

Callista jerked to a stop, causing Bella and Modo to tumble onto the sandy beach. Bella gulped in fresh air, grateful to escape the reek. The fall woke Modo. He hacked up water, then screamed in agony and grabbed his left leg.

"Eira!" Callista screamed. "Take care of these prisoners!"

Eira appeared and belched out fire near the two water-logged captives. "It will be my pleasure."

Bella crawled away from Eira's temporary flame and scooted to Modo's side propping up his shoulder.

Callista gasped for air. "I need to go in—to the water." She shrunk to her normal size and disappeared beneath the surface.

Eira glared at Modo and Bella.

"Lean on me," Bella whispered.

Modo turned toward her and asked loudly, "What did you say?"

Bella bit back a retort when she noticed blood leaking from his left ear. She angled closer and repeated, "Lean on me."

"I'm fine." Modo said as he winced.

"You will be," she encouraged. "I imagine your dive caused damage, and healing will take time. That was a long way down into the ocean."

"You saw that?" Modo's face crinkled as Bella helped him to his feet.

Eira's black pupils were narrow slits in her silver eyes.

She softened her tone. "Come on. Let's try to move away from the shore."

With his left leg and ear injured, they hobbled in silence.

"I show you mercy, and you thank me by running away with this man?" Eira huffed flames skyward. "You can't trust men. They'll hurt you in the end."

Bella frowned.

"Fortunately, those bindings of his didn't hurt me, or I would've fried his smug face for recreation."

Bella glanced at the ocean. "Callista—"

"Callista wanted me to keep you here while she figures out how to get Peter and Aerowyn to notice."

Modo cleared his throat. "I appreciate you not blasting me with your flames."

The dragon huffed.

"But," he continued, "um, why are you helping Callista?"

Eira turned away from Modo. "Remember Bella? I told you the sea witch promised me revenge on those who put me in this body in the first place."

Modo's brows furrowed. "Who is that?"

Eira faced Bella, ignoring Modo. "King Peter and his nasty daughter, Aerowyn." The words rolled disdainfully off her tongue.

Modo's eyes widened. "Aren't you able to kill them with fire? Isn't that what the story, *The Scorned Fae,* is all about?"

Eira yawned lazily. "Bella, not only are men untrustworthy, but this one is naive if he believes everything he reads in books."

"Aerowyn told me that story was true," Bella protested.

Smoke rose from her nostrils. "I told you before, not everything is as it seems. You would be especially ill-advised to believe anything you hear from that loutish fae!" She dug her claws into the sand and rose onto her back legs. "If you stay long enough, maybe I'll tell you the other side of that story. I *can't* kill the enchantress and her father with my flames. Like the Phoenix, they would arise from the ash. Besides, their death doesn't guarantee I would return to my former self which, ultimately is what I want and what Callista promised should I help her."

Modo rubbed his left ear, as if he didn't hear correctly. "Arise from the ash?"

"You know," Bella said hastily, lest the dragon grow cross. "Like a phoenix."

He looked at her blankly.

"A mythical bird that bursts into flame and is reborn from its own ashes," she explained before she turned back to Eira. "But Aerowyn and Peter aren't phoenixes. Do you mean that Isla didn't die when Leia, the dragon, burned her to powders in *The Scorned Fae*? Was Isla reborn?"

Modo looked at Eira and then at Bella. "Remind me again. Who is Isla?"

"Isla was Aerowyn's sister who was killed—at least in the book—by dragon fire. Isla was fae." Bella faced the dragon. "Is Aerowyn's sister still alive?"

Eira, however, didn't answer her questions. Instead, the dragon glowered at Modo. "You know, if I had the ability to read minds after being hexed like Aerowyn can, I would've seen your trick coming and not been temporarily trapped by nets." The dragon sighed, and her breath singed a nearby palm.

"It *is* true I'm fantastic, but I only have two special skills: breathing fire and flying. Both come in handy for scaring away pests, but I can't change forms like Callista or read people's minds like Aerowyn told me she does."

The captain's wince drew Bella's attention. "Modo, you need to get your weight off that leg. Let's go back to my former prison. There are palm fronds I used to sleep on before you rescued me."

Eira laughed. "He's not much of a man. He can't even walk properly, and he let you get kidnapped again so soon after you escaped."

Modo harrumphed, but thankfully chose to remain silent as Bella led the way to her former prison. Eira flattened a new path alongside them, crushing much of the nearby jungle as she stomped.

Desperate to devise a plan of escape, Bella attempted to distract Eira with questions. "Can you tell us what you did to be cursed?"

"No." The dragon snapped, her British accent growing stronger. "That is a personal matter. It is uncouth to ask a lady for intimate information when you barely know each other. We aren't even friends, since you clearly aren't willing to help me return to my former self."

"I was not aware that we needed to," Modo protested.

"Silence!" Eira shouted. "I'm not talking to you, *man*!"

They could not afford to anger the beast, so Bella said calmly, "Captain Modo and I haven't had time to discuss what you needed from me. He's a little in the dark on why Callista kidnapped me."

Eira sat down on her haunches and sighed. "Sorry, I'm a little cantankerous when I need to eat. You know... I could let you go and ignore Callista's desire for revenge *if* you brokered a deal with that impish king."

Bella huffed. "And how are we supposed to do that? I'm tired of being a pawn in the magical creatures' games. I only want to return home and live a normal life. I would even leech off Brooke and Antoine if it meant getting away from all this lunacy."

Modo raised his eyebrows in surprise. Before she could ask him why anyone would be astonished that she would rather not be kidnapped by kraken or witches transformed into sea serpents, Eira said, "You, my dear, have the key to ending all the misery of the creatures King Peter and his daughter cursed. In fact, Callista sent me to spy on the fae on Ageless Isle, I heard why they are using you."

Hope erased Bella's weariness with Eira's revelation. "Why are they using me?"

"Tut, tut. I'm not giving you that information freely."

"What do you want?" Bella's voice hitched.

Worry lines formed between Modo's eyebrows. "Bella, do not believe anything she says."

"Don't tell me what to do!" Bella said under her breath. "I'm not so naive or stupid to believe Eira has my best interests at heart."

He shook his head. "I don't think you are ignorant, but sometimes your curious side outweighs your practical nature, and you act impetuously."

Eira snorted so loudly that the ground shook. Their attention snapped to the mammoth creature to see steam emanating from her nostrils.

"This is delightful!" Eira giggled. "A lover's spat is definitely more entertaining than watching that hag Callista boss around merfolk."

"We're not lovers!" Modo and Bella blurted out together.

"Well, there's clearly some tension between you two, and it doesn't come from hate." She chortled again, and more steam rose.

Modo glared up at the dragon. "Madam, you have this situation all wrong! I was assigned to take Bella to New Orleans alive and in one piece. I care about Bella's safety."

While Bella gaped, he turned to address her. "I'm sorry my attempt to keep you at a distance and avoid the appearance of impropriety—unlike Captain Falcon—gave you the perception that I am indifferent toward you."

"See, I was right." Eira sniggered. "You have *definite* feelings for each other. I should lock you up and leave you alone for a few hours to work it out."

"No!" Bella exclaimed.

"That won't be necessary," Modo added.

"Don't tell me what to do," the dragon mimicked. She pulled the familiar bone-cage from some bushes. "Even if you aren't lovers, I cannot allow you to wander around the island while I hunt. This pen is only for precaution. When I return, perhaps you can tell me how you're going to persuade Aerowyn to change me back to a woman."

Eira lowered the dome-shaped enclosure of bones over them and took to the air.

Bella groaned. She was stuck in the prison again, and this time, the captain was trapped with her. No one would come to save them.

They were on their own.

# Chapter 23

# Captain Modo

M odo couldn't decipher if the bones were human or not.

"Does she eat humans?" Modo turned his good ear toward Bella in case she spoke quietly.

Bella's lips turned slightly upward. "No, she was human and thinks it's cannibalistic."

Modo exhaled. "Good, because I feel like I'm under a covering for a gigantic dragon's dinner plate." He steadied his voice. "I suppose we are back where you were before I rescued you?"

"Yes." Bella's semi-smile disappeared. "Eira will probably be back soon with a rabbit, though without the mermaid's help, we might have to eat it half cooked with dragon-fire." She sighed. "I'm sorry my rescue attempt didn't work."

Modo flinched. "I'm not ungrateful. I'm in pain and worried that once again you're in danger. Thank you for your bravery, regardless of the outcome."

For a few minutes, they were silent.

"You're nothing like Jasper Falcon," she said softly. "But you are confusing, kind, frustrating, snobbish, and sometimes handsome."

"Sometimes?" Modo's heart fluttered. "What does that mean?"

Bella fidgeted with her petticoat, which made Modo realize she was in her undergarments. "Here, you may have this." Modo pulled off his soiled waistcoat and handed it to her.

Bella's cheeks pinkened and she hastily donned his jacket.

"What I mean—" Bella swallowed "—is that there is more to a person than what they look like. We discussed this before. Gorgeous people aren't attractive if their actions are abhorrent. When you helped me and looked out for my best interests, I was attracted to you." Then she looked him in the eye. "Then you ran away from me after I kissed you and well... I agree, it was impetuous and I regret it, but still..."

His head whirled. How was he supposed to respond to that? He'd hoped the whole kiss debacle had been forgotten after the kidnapping. He wanted a second chance and this time he would kiss her back.

He broke their eye contact. "I-I'm sorry for my reaction that day. There were several reasons I didn't respond or return the kiss that I can't share with you."

Bella's face scrunched.

After a few minutes, she asked, "Can you give me at least one of the 'many reasons' you ran like I had a disease?"

"I'm not allowed to say." Which wasn't entirely true, but he wasn't ready to tell her his identity. He couldn't give up yet.

Bella wrapped some stray strands of hair around her finger. "Is that because Aerowyn cursed you? I don't think you're a hideous monster, but you could be a recipient of a different kind of hex."

"Not a hex, but she and I do have an... arrangement," he said. "She did use magic on me."

"Are you allowed to tell me anything about it?"

"Not without breaking the deal. That is partially why I've kept my distance from you." He inhaled then blew out a breath. "It wasn't only an attempt to be proper. You can't discover the agreement I made with Aerowyn."

After a moment, Bella smiled. "Are you allowed to tell me anything to enlighten me?"

"I think we can lift this cage," he said abruptly. After all, escape was more important than figuring out how much he was willing to tell her.

She scowled. "I guess mysteries will remain veiled." She stood and pushed up on the cage. "It's heavier than it looks."

Pain shot through Modo's leg when he stood up, but he turned to keep Bella from seeing his recoil.

"I'll help you lift this time."

Bella gave him a doubtful shrug but nodded.

"I'll count to three," he said, "and on three we'll lift at the same time."

Bella put her hands on the bones and nodded.

"One, two, three."

Grunting they lifted the domed structure. It moved!

If Bella saw how much pain he was in, she would make him stop. They couldn't when they were this close. He braced his leg.

"Again," he said through clenched teeth.

Together, they strained. The cage toppled over. Escape was possible.

Exhilarated, Modo cheered, "Huzzah! I told you so."

Bella laughed. "I haven't heard someone use that expression since—" She stopped and looked at him closely.

"We don't have time to dally," he said, hoping to cover the awkward silence. "We need to leave before Eira returns."

"Last time I fainted from running." Bella palmed the perspiration from her forehead.

"I remember, but I'm in no shape to run. Besides, Eira can fly and see anywhere we go if we're not hidden." Modo rubbed his leg.

"It doesn't matter. She can probably smell exceptionally well with such huge nostrils. Besides, without a boat, there's no way off this island. We need to mask our scent and hide."

"Good thinking."

The lofty trees blocked the sun and sky from their view. They maneuvered haphazardly through the dense, dark greens of vegetation. They couldn't avoid stepping on plants since there wasn't a smoothed-out path under the cover of the trees, but scents of rich soil and exotic flowers soon were overpowered by the stench of death.

Modo set a hand on Bella's arm, silently warning her to proceed with caution. He had found a rotting body in the alley behind his father's pub once, and the reek never left his memory. They neared a strangely shaped plant, and he knew at once where the odor emanated from. The stinky plant loomed above Modo, perhaps ten-feet tall.

Bella gagged. "What's that awful smell?"

He pointed up. "I believe it is this odd-looking plant."

She eyed the vegetation and seemed to consider touching the rancid thing. The outer part of the flower, if that is what it could be called, looked like a gigantic, ribbed tulip-shaped bowl. The lower part was green but lightened to a cream color to the opening, and inside was burgundy, with a tall spike growing out of the middle.

"This could cover our scent if it's not toxic to skin," Bella suggested.

"It would, but besides not knowing if it's poisonous, Eira could smell it a mile away. Perhaps we should look for something more subtle to cover our tracks."

"You're probably right." Bella squinted at the plant. "But it seems like having the smell of death may come in handy for some future purpose."

He paused. She was right.

And that gave Modo an idea on how he could die to save Bella.

# Chapter 24

# Bellarose

"I don't believe you!" Bella gently slapped his arm. "Minutes ago, you told me the plant could be poisonous, and now you want to rub it all over your body? You could die, Fitzwilliam Modo." Tears threatened to escape, so she swallowed hard. "There must be a better way to trick Eira into freeing us but still telling us why King Peter and Aerowyn need me."

He looked straight into her eyes. "I told Aerowyn I would save you, and I meant it. Besides, if this is our last day on earth, I want to remember your face as it is, not covered with plant sludge." He caught her hands. "You truly are the most beautiful woman I have ever seen."

Bella was stunned by his boldness and his statement. He truly thought she was beautiful?

Before she found her voice, he pulled her closer, bridging the gap between them. His lips briefly touched hers. Butterflies fluttered in her stomach, and her body quivered.

His voice was slightly shaky. "I should have done that after you kissed me." His gaze darted between her lips and eyes. He dropped her hands and he gently pushed the loose hair to put it behind her ear. "I never kissed a girl before. And, since this could be our last chance to be honest with each other, I wanted you to know, I do care."

"Your plan will work. I know it will, which means this isn't our last opportunity." Bella's cheeks felt too warm. "I've never kissed anyone before, either." She wiggled her eyebrows. "I think with practice, we could both become experts."

Modo flushed. Silently he smiled, gently took her face into his hands, and lightly kissed her again.

Eira was right, they did care for one another. It was ironic they realized this just before his death.

. . • • ☀ • • . .

Bella screamed loudly, knowing the dragon would find her. "Help me! Please! Somebody, help! Something is wrong with Captain Modo."

Eira landed nearby, crushing all vegetation in her wake. "Girl, I was looking all over for both of you. I didn't realize you could tip over that cage."

"We couldn't. We were attacked by a strange beast that I've never seen before. It threw the prison off us and spewed this thick substance all over the captain. Modo thought if we could get to safety, we would be fine." Bella wiped her eyes. "We were trying to run, but his leg gave out, and then he fell! I tried to look for water but when I returned, he... he..."

Eira's giant nostrils pinched. "Smells like death. Is he breathing? There wasn't enough time for his body to decay, but he definitely stinks like a corpse." The dragon sneezed, blowing small flames in the air. "I imagine the monster that did this was going to return to eat him once he died. That spittle was probably much like a spider web used to trap prey."

Bella covered her eyes and wailed, "He can't be dead. He was my only way home."

"Also, you loved him." Eira snorted. She stooped to check his breathing but couldn't bend her neck that low.

Bella cried louder.

"I don't think he's breathing, but it's hard to see. That awful slime makes him look deceased," Eira said matter-of-factly.

"You make it sound like his death is as common as the weather," Bella protested and proceeded to howl for several minutes.

When she stopped, Eira yawned. Bella frowned into her hands. Do dragons have human emotions? Eira had been a woman before, but maybe the hex had done more than give her scales, a huge jawline, and a protruding nose. Whatever the cause, clearly sympathy wasn't the way to convince Eira to do anything.

Bella turned a sigh into a sob.

"Could you bring him back to his ship to be buried at sea? He's no use to you now. Then you can take me to Ageless Isle, and I'll try to barter a trade with Aerowyn."

The dragon finally looked interested. "What kind of trade?"

"Didn't you say I was valuable? I will explain that I'm willing to do whatever they need me to do in exchange for your freedom from this curse."

Eira's eyes narrowed into slits. "It won't be that simple. If you find out why Aerowyn and Daddy Dearest need you, it may ruin their plan." Her accent thickened. "They won't be willing to risk that." She glowered at Bella.

"They don't need to tell me," Bella said. "They can put me where I should be to continue their scheme. Hopefully there won't be any more interruptions by those they've managed to anger with their curses."

"Callista is still out there," Eira mused. "You may need a different mode of transportation. I think this handsome captain had something to do with the fae's plan, although I guess that's a moot point." Her silver eyes scanned Modo's body. "He's not handsome anymore. I bet you wish you seduced him before he was attacked."

Bella remained silent and turned away from the dragon.

Eira hummed. "I suppose I could bring him back to his ship regardless of how much you help me. Go find something to cover his body so I won't be poisoned by whatever that muck is. Also, don't get poisoned in the process because I need you alive. I'll fly you to the ship, drop him off, and then take you to Ageless Isle."

Bella dashed into the jungle and brought back large banana leaves, which she wrapped around Modo's body. The smelly plant wasn't toxic—Modo had touched it first to make sure—but its sap left a gooey mess, which made him sticky enough for the leaves to adhere. However, she avoided touching it to continue the ruse.

Bella returned to the jungle to find vines, which weren't as strong as she'd hoped.

Eira looked down at Bella. "What are you going to do with all of that?"

"I'll wrap the leaves around Captain Modo so the poison won't touch either of us and then I thought I'd use the vines to wrap around his body and yours to hold him in place." She bit her lip. "But I didn't think about how I was going to hold onto to you."

The dragon puffed out some steam in laughter. "There is no way that vine will hold either of you. He's deadweight." She laughed again. "See what I did there? He's dead and he doesn't move."

Through clenched teeth Bella said, "Yes, I understand."

After Eira stopped spouting steam through her nose, Bella asked, "What do you propose I do to anchor us to your back?"

"I lied about only having the ability to fly and breathe fire. I have a bit of magic also. I can levitate you and the captain to my back and hold you there until I want to let go."

Bella's eyes widened. Even if she had magic, the thought of Eira holding Bella in place while flying so high seemed a bit dangerous, but she didn't have time to panic over the idea as she floated mid-air alongside Modo.

"I can't see what I'm doing. Bella, will you straddle my back and help drape the corpse over my back. Once I feel both of you on top of me, I can concentrate on keeping you in place."

Eira's spine had several ridges poking out. Bella was thankful they were far enough apart for her and Modo to fit in between them. Since the dragon's head was facing forward, she couldn't see Modo help Bella move his body over Eira's back. Even wrapped in leaves his arms were free to move.

Bella called, "I think we're secure." She grabbed onto the dorsal spine for extra insurance. "You may take us to the *Notre Dame*."

"That's in France. I will be delivering the captain to his vessel."

"Modo's ship is also called *Notre Dame*."

"How odd." Eira quirked her head. "I guess even pirates have religious backgrounds."

"Modo isn't a pirate." Bella protested.

"Maybe that explains why he was so proper." Eira clicked her tongue. "It really is too bad he's dead. You would have made an interesting couple."

"I'm sure I don't understand what you're saying," Bella snapped, relieved that Modo had his eyes closed. She was sure her embarrassment would have been evident to anyone watching.

As they lifted, Bella gasped. The air left her lungs temporarily. Flashes of flying on Jasper's ship came back to her, but this was nothing like that experience. Panic seized her chest, and she hung onto Eira. Nothing but supposed magic kept her from falling. The ground grew blurry, and her stomach lurched. The cooler, thinner air had Bella struggling to gulp in oxygen. She kept her eyes shut to keep the vertigo and fear of plunging to her death at bay.

It took mere minutes for Eira to locate the ship. Bella's stomach lurched as the dragon dipped downward despite the smoothness of the movement. Eira's bulky body was surprisingly graceful.

Loud bangs made Bella open her eyes. The ship was firing at them.

Turquoise water stretched as far as the eye could see, and except for the cannon balls plunging into the depths, the ocean was calm.

*Kaboom!*

Another explosion threatened to end all their lives.

Eira dodged right and then left. Each time Bella and Modo held on tightly from fear of slipping into the ocean. Sometimes the dragon blew fire at the projectiles, disintegrating them into dust.

Between blasts Bella screeched, "Stop!"

Finally, Jeb spotted her.

"Cease fire!" Jeb yelled. "Beller is on the dragon!"

The weapons abruptly stilled.

Eira snarled, "Stupid men! You almost got us all killed—" she chortled "—your captain is already dead."

The men gasped.

"I'll lower your captain onto the ship so you can bury him at sea as a favor to Bella, but you may want a net to catch him. He's a mess."

Westley reacted quickly, "Secure the net men!"

Sailors scurried to put the mesh in place. Bella's muscles tensed. She wasn't strong enough to lower him gently, and the fall might kill him. Modo opened one eye and nodded.

Bella grunted as she pretended to push Modo towards the web, but he aided her by shoving himself off the dragon.

Bella held her breath as he landed in the net and lay lifelessly still. She squeezed her eyes shut at the thought of Modo experiencing more pain or worse—death.

"Beller, go ahead and jump, "Jeb shouted. "We'll catch you!"

"I'm not coming." Bella's throat was hoarse. "Eira is going to take me to Ageless Isle to broker a deal with the enchantress. I asked her to return Modo to you in exchange for my cooperation."

"Pish-posh!" Eira snorted. "Say goodbye and let us be on our way!"

"Goodb—"

Eira lifted into the clouds before Bella could finish.

It was probably better this way, but Bella wanted to cry. Despair took hold. She had no control over her current situation and already missed Modo's quirks.

Knowing no one else had to be harmed kept the tears at bay. Jeb probably would have attacked the dragon to save Bella, which would have only ended in disaster.

Keeping her eyes shut, Bella drew a deep, steadying breath and peeled off Modo's jacket. Between the shirt, which she used as a cleaning rag, and the moisture in the air, she rubbed away the stickiness on her skin. She wasn't able to completely avoid getting some of the goo on her while she wrapped his body. When she finished removing the foul-smelling sap, Bella tossed the coat into the air, and the current carried it away.

Eira's muscles tightened under Bella as the air whipped harder on her face. The dragon might have been flying faster, but she was afraid to open her eyes to see. The last time she peeked, she nearly vomited.

What could she possibly say that would convince Aerowyn or Peter to reverse their spell on Eira? It was a longshot, but she had to try since the dragon had rescued her from Callista. The wind nearly propelled her off Eira, and the air grew thinner and wilder.

Bella held on tightly repeating, "I will survive. I will survive."

Eira finally spoke. "In the king's name, will you please be quiet? You're annoying me."

"How much farther is it?"

"I'm not sure." Eira sighed. "The fae must have put an invisible wall around the whole blooming island to prevent unwelcomed visitors from discovering it. When I spied on them, it was easier to find."

Bella opened her eyes and squinted ahead—not looking down. "That triggers a memory. When I visited before, we had Peter with us." Bella moaned. "What if we need magic to find it?"

Eira screeched, which sounded more animal than human. "Do you recall any navigational instructions from Peter?"

Bella focused on the memory. "I think he said it is located the second star to the right." She tucked her bottom lip in. "Does that help?"

"To the right of what?"

*Keow—ha-ha-ha-ha—Keow*

*Crunch. Gulp.*

"What was that?" At the strange sound, Bella's eyes popped open.

Eira burped. "Pardon me. It was a seagull. Or rather, it was a snack—the perils of flying near a dragon."

Bella shuddered and shut her eyes.

"So, what were you saying about a star?" Eira inquired.

Bella swallowed hard. "Peter told me it was a star named Cigam, the most dazzling object in the night sky. He based his navigation on it. The island is located directly in line with the second star to the right of Cigam."

"If you haven't noticed," Eira said dryly, "it's daytime, and there aren't any stars out. How are we supposed to find the most dazzling one?"

"Maybe we have to wait until it gets dark?"

"I don't want to wait. Callista will come looking for you or Modo. We need to find it now."

Bella sucked in air. Without magic, it could be a futile search, but then a thought occurred to her.

"Do you have exceptional hearing?"

Eira huffed. "Yes, of course. Why?"

Bella rolled her eyes even though the dragon couldn't see her. "Listen for some boys using the word 'huzzooee'."

"Huzzo—what?" Eira snorted. "That's not even a word."

Bella chuckled. "I thought the same thing when I heard it, but the Lost Boys use it a lot. I think it is their word for *attack* or *hooray*, but I never asked."

"Who are the Lost Boys?"

Bella smiled. "Leprechauns on Ageless Isle."

"Leprechauns are not boys. They are little men with pots of gold in Ireland, and they are entirely fictional."

"Aren't dragons fictional too?" Bella sniggered. "Until Aerowyn pulled me into her scheme, I thought a lot of mythical creatures were imaginary, and now I know none of them are."

Another bird squawked and Bella's muscles stiffened as she recalled the previous seagull's demise.

However, Eira ignored the fowl and continued, "I suppose. I'm flying around with scales. I can still feel my smooth skin. I was beautiful."

"Ignore the sea. Ignore the distance," Bella told herself. She squeezed her eyes tightly shut and tried to picture Eira the woman. She couldn't manage it, so she continued.

"The leprechauns don't look like fairy tales say they do. I think they are normal boys who were abandoned and forgotten. Peter gives them a place to live and gifts them with magic. There are all kinds of dangerous creatures and intruders on the island, and Jericho, the head lost boy, told me Peter gave them supernatural abilities to stay safe."

Earlier screaming made Bella's voice raspy. "The boys must pass a test to see if they are suited for life on Ageless Isle. Peter puts them in good homes to be adopted if they don't pass the tests."

"You make him sound kind and generous. He isn't." Flames came out of Eira's mouth.

The heat made Bella open her eyes briefly. It seemed the very thought of Peter literally fired the dragon up from the inside out.

Eira continued. "He's foul and menacing. He curses anyone who doesn't agree with his standards of living. He's a dictator who doesn't give anyone a chance to be free!"

"I don't know what to think of the enchantress and her father." Bella tightened her hands around one of Eira's dorsal spikes. "I don't trust them." She huffed. "But they have always been kind to me. I fear them and wonder what their ulterior motives really are."

"Wise girl. Now please stop talking so I can listen for voices."

Eira flew through the air like a dancer gliding on a smooth floor.

While Bella kept her eyes shut, the fluid motion relaxed her. Opening them once to peek at the islands below, dizziness and nausea nearly knocked her off the dragon's back.

Perhaps it was best, she decided, to shut her lids and her mouth and allow Eira to hone in on signs of human life.

# Chapter 25

# Captain Modo

M odo watched Eira through barely open eyes. As soon as she disappeared beyond the clouds, he untangled himself from the net while sitting upright. After a few gasps, the crew cheered.

Westley addressed him, "Captain, we've been worried about you and Miss Bella."

Jeb asked, "What 'app'n?"

A sailor brought Modo a bucket of water and a sponge. He hobbled over to the bucket and washed off the noxious smelling plant along with the blood from his damaged ear. While he cleaned himself, he explained to the men and the newest members of their crew, the cursed merfolk, what had happened and told them where Eira was taking Bella and why.

No one thought it was a good idea, even though the plan had been their only way off the island.

"Does anyone know how we journey back to Ageless Isle?" Modo asked.

"No sir," Westley responded. "It took pixie dust or magic to fly the ship there."

"Eira believed Ageless Isle was close to where we were held captive." Modo wiped his face with a towel a crewman handed him. "I kept my eyes open when she flew me to the ship. I think I can find it." Modo beckoned to the sailing master, Magnus. "You're with me."

"Cap'n," Jeb said. "I wan' to see Beller safe. I'm 'ere to 'elp." Jeb saluted Modo.

"Since you've been to the island." Modo turned to look at Jeb. "You may help us map the course. Maybe you can remember something about the island that will help."

Jeb smiled widely. "Thank ya Cap'n. I'll do me bes'."

Modo limped to his cabin where his maps and navigational tools lay. Magnus, who was responsible for plotting courses followed him, with Jeb and Westley close behind. Modo laid out the maps, thankful again for his new body and the seafaring knowledge Aerowyn had given him. He needed to succeed on this mission. Uneasiness competed with the gratitude. If only she had given him the ability to defeat the monsters, she and her father, Peter had cursed.

Using the men's knowledge, Modo charted their path, and gave Magnus the information needed. The small group departed from Modo's quarters, and the captain and sailing master proceeded to the helm to set the course.

The former mermaid with pink hair grabbed the papers out of Magnus's hands. He protested, but she held up her palm. For some reason, the man fell silent. As she studied the maps, a scowl descended on her face. Turning to a merman with blue hair, she waved her hands.

The blue-haired merman said, "Captain."

Modo startled. "You can talk?"

"Yes."

"When we were working out a plan to rescue Bella, we thought none of you had tongues. How are you able to talk?"

"Some of us pretended to be mute," he confessed, though he kept his eyes on Modo's. "Eira has a keen sense of hearing."

"But we were talking..." Modo shrugged. "Very well. What is your name?"

"I am Philip." He gestured at the pink-haired mermaid. "My wife, Syrena, doesn't have a tongue, so I will speak for her. She has visited Ageless Isle."

Modo turned to Syrena. "Can you lead us there?"

"She can, but you will run into the invisible wall." Philip put his hand on Syrena's shoulder.

Modo wiped away perspiration from his forehead. "Invisible wall?"

Syrena made more hand gestures.

Philip explained, "King Peter created a mirage to appear as miles of ocean to block ships from accidentally finding the island. Only by flying can you reach Ageless Isle."

Modo grunted. "Oh, is that all?"

"I have some of that pixie dust that helped us fly the *Black Fear II*," Magnus volunteered. "I noticed some on me shirt from the first time our ship flew. I bottled it up for a souvenir."

"Really? Show me. I've heard of a flying vessel, but I haven't seen anything like that," Modo said.

Magnus pulled out his small jar from his pants pocket and he held it up as if it were a rare prize.

Modo turned to the blue-haired merman. "Philip, is that enough to fly this ship?"

Philip shook his head. "I don't think so."

"Wha' abou' our 'appy fought?" Jeb inquired.

"What do happy thoughts have to do with the pixie material or flying?" Modo asked.

Syrena made more signs to Philip, who translated for the rest of them. "Supposedly, it takes the pixie fairy's dust and everyone thinking happy thoughts to lift the ship, but Syrena doesn't think what you concentrate on makes a difference. She suspects Peter used it as a way to see what made everyone happy, since he can read minds."

Modo narrowed his eyes. "How does she know so much about Peter and this magical dust?"

"She was Aerowyn's friend, ages ago. Callista was jealous of their friendship and cursed my wife by taking away her tongue and fins." The merman's voice tightened. "It doesn't take much to anger that witch, but of course in my attempt to stop Callista from hurting Syrena, I was cursed too. At least we were able to be together on that island, but that's a story for another time."

Modo wrung his hands. They couldn't afford to waste the dust if raising the ship didn't work, but his options were limited. Bella would require help, and Aerowyn appointed him to be her rescuer. It didn't matter if she loved him. All that mattered was her safe return to New Orleans, her new home. Surely, Brooke and Antoine would welcome her back. Love would eventually find her, and she would live happily ever after like the stories she read.

"Captain Modo!" Everyone jumped at the squeaky, high-pitched voice.

Modo didn't recognize the sailor. He was short and quite slight, and his blonde hair almost blinded Modo in the sunlight. Odd. He knew everyone on the ship. That was part of what a captain did.

"I don't believe I know your name, sailor," he said, trying to keep suspicion out of his voice. "Who are you?"

"I'm, um, I'm Till. I'm nobody, sir. Just one of the crew that keeps this ship in tip-top shape. Anyway, see my jar?" Till held out a huge jar of the sparkly substance. His supply far outweighed the sailing master's.

Modo's eyes widened. "How did you get so much? The *Black Fear* sank and the *Black Fear II* disappeared."

"I- I- um- I- shook off all the sails at night and swept up any I could find." Till darted his eyes downward and then sideways. "I thought I could sell it for a profit during shore leave."

Till's story didn't sound like the whole truth, but Modo needed that pixie dust.

"All right men. Help spread this powder. Philip, can you translate Syrena's directions and lead us to the island?"

"Yes."

The crew scurried around raising sails and singing songs from their pirate days. Excitement buzzed through the men at the prospect of flying. For some, it would be the first time experiencing such magic, but for others it would be a repeat of when Peter took them to Ageless Isle after the *Black Fear* sank.

The chance to rescue Bella made Modo's heart thump a little faster inside his chest, but so far, nothing in this journey had been easy. It was likely this wouldn't be trouble-free, either.

# Chapter 26

# Bellarose

B ella's eyes were tightly shut when Eira declared, "I think I hear the witch."

You hear Callista?" Fear forced Bella to look down. She couldn't see the chartreuse snake, and vertigo immediately made the world spin, so she closed her eyes again.

"Not Callista." Eira clucked her tongue. "I mean Aerowyn. I loathe that nasty witch."

*An opinion,* Bella thought, *that should be kept to herself.*

Bella gulped. "I hope that means she's near and you can take me directly to Aerowyn instead of the leprechauns."

The dragon began her descent, and Bella's stomach tickled during the drop. Familiar, spicy scents prompted Bella to open her eyes. Eira flew over a colorful woodland of crimson-leafed cinnapepper trees. The enthralling scenery temporarily minimized Bella's fears.

"The witch's grating voice is getting louder."

An array of purple, orange, pink, and blue leaves danced below the dragon, who glided to land on a field of wildflowers that bordered the uniquely-colored foliage.

"I saw stairways leading up to those strange trees." Eira said. "That's where the witch's voice was the strongest. Though I want to squash the mistress of evil, I doubt that will break my curse. I need her alive to undo the damage she has caused." She flattened her body over the ground. "I can't get you any closer, or I'll damage the fae's homes."

"You have amazing vision! I only saw those crazy-colored trees. Are you going to wait for me to make a deal with her?"

"Yes." Eira positioned her body for Bella's exit. "I'll wait."

Bella attempted to crawl down but instead Eira floated Bella up and away from the spiked back and then placed her on the ground. Bella straightened her soiled petticoat, and started toward the multi-hued timberland.

She stopped and tilted her head to make eye contact with Eira. "How should I approach Aerowyn? Do you have any suggestions?"

"There are many un-lady-like words I wish to say, but I don't think that will help my case any more than squishing her would." Eira ground her talons into the field. "Say what you feel is necessary."

When Bella entered the dense forest, she immediately saw the stairways Eira had spotted from the sky. They protruded from the trunks and led to oddly shaped structures formed around the trees. Bella searched the forest for Aerowyn's home. Within seconds, a large black wolf bounded down the stairs of a blue-leafed tree. She froze. The wolf approached her cautiously, then began wagging its tail, and making happy noises.

"Gerard, is that you?"

His thick black tail wagged rapidly which she took as a yes, and soon Aerowyn floated in front of Bella. The enchantress didn't seem to walk, but rather drifted gracefully across the forest floor over the moss and greenery that covered the rich soil like a green carpet being rolled out for its queen.

"Bella, you made it." Aerowyn's tone was musical and soothing, not grating as the dragon had described it, but the enchantress's violet eyes expressed something other than pleasant greetings. "I have been expecting you."

"I suppose I shouldn't be surprised," Bella responded, "but how *did* you know I was coming here?"

"Although I can't be everywhere at once, I knew about your kidnapping experiences. Captain Modo rescued you the first and second times, but you risked your life to help him. I don't know if I should admire your heroism or criticize your recklessness."

Bella put her hands on her hips and glared at the sorceress. "And I don't know if I should be angry that you've put me in these situations in the first place or be infuriated that ultimately it's your fault I'm here."

Gerard whined and nosed at Bella's leg, but when she looked down at him, his attention was fixed on Aerowyn.

The enchantress finally spoke. "Gerard informs me that your impertinence and redundant comments are an indication that you feel insulted. Is this a defense mechanism?"

"No," Bella said through clenched teeth. "It's my way of criticizing you without being too crass. I'm trying to control my temper."

"My, my, you are a spirited thing. I suppose being captured multiple times can put one in a mood."

Bella's fingers moved into a fist. She whispered, "Keep calm," to herself, then drew in a deep breath and put on an artificial smile. "However, I didn't come here to insult you. I came to ask that you free Eira from her curse and allow me to go back to New Orleans to live a peaceful life. Far away from magic."

Aerowyn's eyes became tea-colored and Bella saw the enchantress's haughtiness evaporate. "Trust me. I want to do all of that." Aerowyn spread out her hands. "But I can't."

"You can't? What's that supposed to mean?"

Gerard made a mournful sound.

"I can't reverse the curses I've put on others. Once the magic is set in motion, it must run its course." Aerowyn's shoulders slumped. "The more I discover of my father's misjudgments and missteps, the more regrets I have for following his mission of ridding the world of selfishness."

"What do you mean?"

"It's a long story. Walk with me." Without waiting to see if Bella followed, Aerowyn turned down a mossy path. Bella jogged to catch up, but Gerard was already at the enchantress's side. "As you know, I have been hexing people using the spells my father taught me to use. He said that once payment is made, all will be restored, but I'm beginning to believe that isn't true. The fairy tales have been unwritten and twisted to the degree that even when Gerard sacrificed himself for his brother, it wasn't enough to permanently reverse the curse." She rested her hand on the wolf's head. "That is only one example."

"Why involve me? I have no magic and barely any heroic skills."

"Why don't I explain everything after you wash up, change into clean clothes, and eat? I have all that you need in my abode."

"Eira is waiting for an answer." Bella reminded her. "Do you think it is wise to keep her waiting?"

"Oh, that's right. She isn't pleasant even on a good day." Aerowyn's eyes returned to violet. "The thing is, I can't risk her wrath."

"She won't kill you if that is what's worrying you."

"Are you sure?" Aerowyn shook her head. "If I die, this mess may never get fixed."

"I think her desire to return to being a human is greater than her longing for revenge," Bella assured.

"The truth is…" Aerowyn crossed her arms. "My father, Peter, cast the curse on Eira—not me. She blames me for turning her into a dragon, but I had nothing to do with it. She needs to stop meddling, and go back to her home, Terradraco."

Gerard barked.

A familiar male voice spoke into Bella's mind: *Please convince Eira to return to home and not harm Aerowyn.*

She startled. Looking from the wolf to the enchantress, Bella said, "Did Gerard talk to me, or did I imagine it?"

Aerowyn stared at Gerard and then nodded. "He did, and that isn't normal. He isn't supposed to be able to speak to anyone telepathically but the fae. He is supposed to have the ability to talk mentally to Father and me, but not to a mere human. Maybe Father was right about you."

"Right about what?"

"I will explain, but it's part of that long story."

*Please get Eira to leave. Aerowyn will open up more if a potential assassin isn't spying on her.*

Bella's eyes went wide. "He spoke to me again. Did you hear that?"

"No." Aerowyn narrowed her eyes at him. "What is he saying?"

*Don't tell her.*

"He told me not to tell you," Bella said before she could stop herself. "I mean... I'm going to go back to Eira and convince her to return to her kingdom. I doubt she'll believe my explanation, but it's worth a try."

Bella wiped her wet palms onto her petticoat. Her swirling imagination crafted the worst scenarios possible, and her head pounded. She took shallow breaths. One misstep, and Bella could end up a pile of ash—or worse, a cursed creature.

Bella returned to Eira who lay on the ground with closed eyes.

"Don't bother to sneak up on me. I know you're there. My ears are designed to help me catch prey."

"I wasn't sneaking. It looked like you were asleep, and I didn't want to startle you. Singed hair doesn't look good on me."

Bella would have sworn that Eira almost smiled, a human expression Bella didn't expect.

"I heard everything you and the witch discussed. Like I said, my hearing is extraordinary. However, I didn't hear what the dog said to you." The dragon sat up. "And I wasn't sleeping. I was resting my eyes and practicing my breathing exercises. It is to quiet my temper, so I don't set this whole island on fire." Bella didn't know how to respond, but before she figured out what to say, Eira sighed. "I'm rather tired of being a dragon."

Bella dared to get close to Eira and then tenderly put her human hand onto the dragon's claw. "I'm sorry you have had to bear this curse for so long." She backed away to look into Eira's eyes. "Since you heard everything, you know I came here to beg you to return to your home and wait for your hex to be lifted."

"Yes, I did." Smoke rose from her nostrils. "I also heard her say she had nothing to do with my curse. How pathetic. She has the same powers King Peter has, and I say she's guilty by association. Who's going to teach the fae a lesson in humility? I know she hears what I'm saying, so"—Eira increased the volume of her voice—"Aerowyn, hear this: anyone who sets themselves up as judge and jury over sin, should take a good hard look in the mirror before casting the first hex. They may find they deserve worse than any of their victims."

"It's horrible that you've been wronged." Bella lifted her hand to her chest. "And I agree with you. I once was prideful and thought I was better than anyone. It took the death of my parents and being thrown into poverty to really see myself. We don't have to face our faults while we're busy pointing out everyone else's, and eventually those mistakes have consequences. Be patient, Eira. Vindication is possible, and it may be in a form you don't expect."

Eira lowered her chin, and her smile reached her silver eyes. "How does one so young get so wise?"

Bella's heart broke a little more as the words reminded her of losing Quinn and her parents, so she said almost lightly, "I'll blame it on being abducted multiple times and losing everyone I love."

"I might have lost everyone I love too." Eira's eyes welled with tears. They think I'm dead, but they'd be frightened of me now anyway. Dragons might have bad reputations, but we're not all ruthless murderers."

"For now, though, can you return home and wait? And... you need to stop teaming up with Callista. She isn't going to help you." Bella once again placed her hand over the creature's claw.

Eira sniffed. "I agree about that one. She's nastier than I. Her vendetta against the fae runs much deeper than mine."

Bella nodded and released her touch.

"I will leave." The dragon stood while stretching her wings. "Remember that you promised to help me. I will eventually expect payment."

"I will remember."

Bella stepped away to give Eira's wings room to move. She lifted into the air. Though dragons were always ugly, scaled creatures in Bella's books, Eira had a grace about her, and her white iridescent hide was as regal as diamonds embedded in a crown.

She watched the dragon disappear into the sky, then, yawning she trudged to Aerowyn's tree house and climbed the stairs. Gerard rested on a fluffy cushion on the floor, but Aerowyn stood in the middle of the room with a strange expression on her face.

Bella was sure this adventure was going to be the death of her, but until then she would put on a brave face. She straightened her shoulders and smiled.

# Chapter 27

# Captain Modo

S oaring under the white-saucer moon amongst puffs of clouds rather than on water made every object in the sky seem touchable and near. As Modo stood at the prow under the star-studded heavens, hope for Bella's safety and for her future preoccupied him. Bumps formed on his arms from the wind chill, but he didn't notice. Once Bella was free from the fae and safe, once she was back in his care, he was determined to woo her under this brilliant firmament.

Westley startled Modo out of his awake-dreams. "Captain, the men were wondering if you could read them a story. With Bella gone, they've been missing the nightly tales. Most of them can't read and rather be read to anyway."

"It would be my honor." Modo smiled. "Bella's books always make her feel nearby."

Westley nodded. "Aye, Captain. That's probably why the men want to keep the routine in her absence."

The two men strolled to the main deck. Modo inhaled deeply, enjoying the peculiar scent that might have been magic emanating from the pixie-dust covered sails. They sparkled supernaturally under the moonlight, giving the upper decks of the ship an otherworldly feel. It kept Bella in his forethoughts. Bella attracted magic.

A group of men and merfolk were already gathered on the deck and water barrels.

Jeb handed a book to Modo. "Read dis one. I fancy the cover."

The emerald outer leather casing reminded Modo of Bella's eyes. He wondered if that was why Jeb chose it, or if it was because the girl imprinted on the cover was similar to Bella. Modo sat on a bench Bella always used. He inhaled the smell of leather and paper as he opened the book titled *Lost Girl*.

Modo began, "Once upon a time—"

"Avast!" the crow's nest watchman yelled. "There's a dragon to the port side!"

Heads turned toward the direction he pointed, and Modo's heart sank. A white, iridescent scaled dragon flew without a rider, the glowing moon as her backdrop. A blaze of reds and yellows blew from her mouth, and she disappeared into the blackened clouds.

Gasps and curses followed the spectacle as the men mumbled amongst themselves speculating at what seeing Eira meant. Despair flooded Modo. Had the dragon incinerated the enchantress and Bella? They needed to get to that island!

"Syrena! Does anyone know where that mermaid is?"

The pink-haired woman approached the captain with Phillip by her side.

Panic filled Modo's booming voice. "Do you know any way we can get to Ageless Isle faster?"

She gestured at Phillip.

"She suggested," Phillip interpreted, "that you should find a wind current that can push the sails faster."

"Yes," Modo sighed, "That is what we're trying to do, but does she have any other suggestions?"

Syrena shook her head.

Modo's resolve to rescue Bella became a fire in his stomach. The angst of potentially losing her forever created a physical pain.

He had to bring Bella to safety. She had to be aboard the *Notre Dame*. She had to. There was no other option.

# Chapter 28

# Bellarose

B ella scanned Aerowyn's domicile while they talked. When she first approached the dwelling, fear and intimidation loomed over her. But, once she entered the quaint abode, a woodsy, floral scent calmed her nerves. Wildflowers in warm hues of blue, lavender, and cream grew from the inner walls. The comfortable furniture and décor were homey—unexpected in a place where a powerful enchantress lived. The atmosphere, and even Aerowyn, put Bella at ease until she learned why the fae involved her in their schemes.

"Go down the hall to your right. You will find everything you need. After you've cleaned up, meet me in the dining room."

Bella was too tired to question her, though she hoped for a basin of water to wash off the grime, to her surprise the room was identical to the one aboard the *Notre Dame*. The large bed was draped with a luxurious white coverlet embroidered with red satin roses. The plush pillows and soft looking mattress called to her weary body—but even the fully loaded shelves of books couldn't stimulate Bella. Off to the corner was a bathtub that was filling with rose scented steaming water.

Bella's filthy clothes evaporated from her body, and she blushed, even though there were no windows or prying eyes. Aerowyn's magic might be atrocious when performing curses, but it could also provide respite. She gladly stepped into the opulent tub and let the warm water soothe her.

A soft sponge wiped off the days of muck. A bucket of water poured over her hair to rid it of sand from the near drowning and island captivity. Magic anticipated her every need.

When Bella was thoroughly clean and dry, another invisible force floated a dress in front of her. She stepped into it, and a warm wind gently dried her hair. A brush stroked each tendril to smooth out the tangles and curls.

It felt good to be clean.

After Bella was fully dressed and her hair set into soft curls around her face, the scents of roasted meat and baked bread made Bella's mouth water, and her stomach growl in anticipation. It took only a few steps to return to the dining room, where Aerowyn sat at a table covered with delicious-looking food.

The sight, however, gave Bella pause. She had read that one should never eat food from a fairy. Would this feast manipulate her mind and make her hallucinate?

Longing to eat, she sat down at the table but looked skeptically at the steaming bowls of vegetables and meats.

Gerard padded up to her side and nuzzled her.

*Go ahead. This isn't fairy food from the silly stories you talk about all the time. It's safe. Aerowyn needs your help, but only if you willingly give it. She can't force you.*

"My stories aren't silly," Bella protested. "What would you know anyway, Mr. Obtuse?"

"Is he speaking to you again?" Aerowyn's lips pursed. "I'm really surprised he's able to do that without me hearing too. I can read your mind, like he obviously can"—she eyed Gerard crossly—"but I was trying to give you privacy."

"He never understood my love for books. He may have become less arrogant, but he's still a toad."

*Toad! I haven't done anything recently to bring out such insults. You could only be so lucky.*

Bella sniggered. "You did call my books silly, which is a very toad-like thing to say."

*I miss our banter, even if you are so oddly in love with books.*

"I knew being a wolf for months wouldn't totally erase your ego." She grinned at the wolf, then teased, "Besides insulting my love of reading, Gerard thinks I suspect your food is enchanted. I will eat it just to spite him."

Gerard growled quietly and sat on the ground by the table.

Scowling, Aerowyn eyed him and then Bella. "Are you ready to hear what I know?"

Bella put several small portions of food on her plate.

The enchantress smirked. "I know you're hungry. Go ahead and take all the food you can eat. This isn't a test on proper etiquette."

Bella scooped larger portions and in between bites of the delectable food said, "I'm ready to hear all you can tell me."

"My father's mission to curse all the selfish people in the world was ultimately started by my mother's death," Aerowyn paused. "Because she was human."

Bella frowned. "I knew that about your mother. Peter shared that much with me."

"Yes, and he also told you that we left the Kingdom of Magic to live here on Ageless Isle because of my sister Isla's death by dragon fire, which is in that book you love so much."

Bella nodded.

*Of course, it is in one of your books.* Gerard teased. Bella glowered at him.

"But did my father tell you that he was the one who created the dragons in the first place?"

Bella's jaw dropped. "No, he never told me that."

"I guess he wouldn't admit that detail, because that would make him partially to blame for Isla's death." Aerowyn's lips tightened.

"Eira alluded to the fact that maybe your sister didn't die." Bella looked up from her plate. "It confused me, but she told me not to believe everything I read in books."

Aerowyn poured a clear, bubbly liquid from a golden pitcher into her goblet. It reminded Bella of something her parents drank at parties, but the memory was flawed because the whole setting was unfamiliar. Quickly Bella finished her water to shake off the peculiar memory and held out her glass, but within seconds her goblet filled with still water again. The beverage Aerowyn drank probably wasn't fit for humans.

"I know nothing about Eira's gossip, but that is something I need to investigate." The enchantress took a sip. "Father was so broken-heart-ed over Mother's death that he wanted to die. Our history told us that only magical fire can kill an immortal, so he created dragons." She set her glass down and folded her hands. "He changed his mind about wanting to die, but the dragons were already multiplying."

*And I thought my father had issues*, Gerard added.

Bella shushed him, and then said, "I imagine the dragons, along with other hexed creatures have done a lot of damage in the world."

"Yes, and since Father and I are immortals with the ability to per-form magic, we can travel through time and dimensions to fully see the damage."

Bella glanced at Gerard, who grunted as if to say that Aerowyn's words were nonsensical to him also.

"Though intriguing, what you're telling me is mostly confusing, and you haven't told me why you're involving me in your schemes."

"The point is," the enchantress continued, "you know a lot of fairy tales, and we need your knowledge plus imagination. We have seen the origins of stories through our travels, and we know the original tales no longer exist. Father and I meddled too much."

Aerowyn put her palms over her eyes, then clasped her hands on the table. "By adding dragons and sea witches into the stories, we changed folklore's history."

"But how can my knowledge help you with any of this?"

"Father thinks if you have a happy ending, you'll repair some of the tales."

Tired of Aerowyn's unclear explanations, Bella protested, "How can my happy ending do that?"

"He wasn't clear on that exactly." Aerowyn sighed. "I know he lied to me about other things, so I'm still figuring out what is true and what isn't."

"I'm sorry." Bella frowned.

Aerowyn's brows knitted together. "Sorry for what?"

"That you can't trust your own father. I'm familiar with that after my father squandered away the family wealth and lied about why we fled to America."

Tears rose in Aerowyn's eyes, but she wiped the moisture away and gulped her beverage down. "My explanations are confusing because I'm not completely sure of everything Father is doing. He said he's using you to repair the fairy tales. At first, I thought he would lock you up in a room to re-write the damaged stories since you know the original ones before they were changed, but now I hate to say it..."

*Say it, I already read your thoughts on this, and I will tell Bella if you don't.*

"I heard what Gerard said." Bella swallowed, and even though her nerves disagreed with her words, she continued. "Go ahead and tell me. One of you might as well let me know."

The enchantress drew a deep breath. "I believe that to reverse everything he has done; Father will cast a once-for-all magic spell to sacrifice you."

Bella's eyes widened and she covered her mouth with her hand.

"I'm not familiar with a hex like that," Aerowyn said in a rush, "but I recall something about it from our ancient manuscripts."

*It has something to do with your happy ending. He needed you to have a happily-ever-after like the fairy tales you talk about, but it involved—*

"Gerard, you said too much. She won't experience it if she knows about it."

*If it will ultimately kill her, does that matter?*

Bella gasped. "Kill me? You mean my happy ending would end my life?"

"Not necessarily." Aerowyn held up both hands. "Bella, don't panic. Gerard is taking the word literally. It never means death in books."

Bella choked. She sipped some water, but it didn't dissolve the lump in her throat. Dying to repair fairy tales was heroic but scared her senseless.

Gerard nuzzled up against Bella's leg. *No, I won't let that happen.*

Aerowyn reached out and patted Bella's hand. "There is no reason for you to worry about your fate. To my knowledge, Father only needs you to fulfill your fairy-tale-like destiny, and the stories will mend themselves."

Bella moaned. "That seems a little far-fetched. Besides, how am I supposed to do that? I keep getting kidnapped, and I'm relatively sure that isn't part of anyone's happiness."

"I know. We've been unable to control some of the villains my father helped create." The enchantress shook her head. "I need to get you back on the *Notre Dame* with Captain Modo so you can be on your way to New Orleans as originally planned. That should lead you to your fate."

*That is an insane idea. It didn't work before, so what will stop Callista from ruining the plan again?*

"Gerard has a point." Bella folded her hands to keep them from shaking. "I don't want to argue with an enchantress who knows more about magic, but as long as Callista is out there, don't you think I might be kidnapped again? She and Eira know I'm valuable to Peter and will stop at nothing to exchange me for freedom from the curses he placed upon them."

Aerowyn's forehead wrinkled and she closed her eyes for a moment. "You are probably correct, but there are only two ways for you to travel back to Louisiana to fulfil your purpose. Whether by sea or air, both involve Captain Modo's ship."

"Speaking of Captain Modo," Bella began, then paused. She didn't want to ask a question that might stir up the enchantress's anger, but she had to know. This was her chance. "Out of curiosity, why did you use his ship instead of another one to rescue me from the pirates in the first place?"

Aerowyn's eyes kept changing colors. The woman clearly struggled to steady her reactions.

"Bella, I can't tell you why Modo was chosen because..." She exhaled. "It's not for you to know."

Bella studied the fae, then leaned back and crossed her arms. "You mean I can't know my future."

"Yes."

"In that case, give Modo a bunch of pixie dust and help the *Notre Dame* fly us all the way to Louisiana. I think we have a better chance in the air than on sea."

Gerard narrowed his eyes. *While she travels to New Orleans, Aerowyn, you ought to uncover the secret magic Peter wishes to use on Bella. You need to explain why you followed your father to your people. They might help you discover the truth, if it will end his tyranny.*

Bella stared at the wolf in shock. How did he have the audacity to call Aerowyn's father a tyrant to her face? Gerard kept his eyes on the enchantress.

"I'm not helping to end anything. I'm only fixing injustices," Aerowyn protested. "But you're right. I should go to them for help. They may not cooperate with me, but they won't hurt me. Until I try, I won't know. The problem is that I must keep Bella safe while I figure this out. If she doesn't fulfill her destiny, I don't know what to do next."

"I know you can't tell me what my great ending is, but since it requires the *Notre Dame*, it must involve Modo. That means you're looking at the wrong solution." Bella frowned.

"Why do you think that?"

"We've only managed to cooperate once, but then, we were separated. Besides, that was when we were alone on an island trying to escape a dragon. I'm sure once we're on the ship together, he'll go back to his stuffy old ways."

*You need to drop all the asinine, romantic notions you got from fictional books.*

Bella glared at the wolf. "I'll tell you what's asinine, but I would shorten the word to—"

"Don't mock Gerard," Aerowyn interjected. "He wasn't taught how to properly woo young ladies. But I will say that Captain Modo's stuffiness is his way of protecting his own secrets and insecurities. Maybe during the journey back to Louisiana, you'll discover who the real Modo is."

"He has nothing to be insecure about, even though he did tell me he had never kissed anyone before, and that seemed unbelievable."

Aerowyn's lips upturned. "You've seen ships fly and sea witches create typhoons. A young man who has never been kissed shouldn't be on your list of preposterous things."

"I suppose you're correct, but he's so hands—" She caught herself, but her blush probably gave her away.

Gerard made a chuffing noise, as if he were laughing. Bella glowered at the wolf.

"Then it's settled. We get you to the *Notre Dame*, and you make your way to New Orleans. I shall appeal to the fae myself." Aerowyn stood. "Though, perhaps you should rest for a few minutes before we leave."

Would Bella have to face Quinn again in Louisiana? Could she forget the connection of souls and hearts she had with him? Fitzwilliam Modo had begun to heal her pain when he replaced Quinn as her protector and friend, but going back to New Orleans would freshen all the memories she had shared with Quinn.

If her happy ending was tied in with the *Notre Dame*, then she suspected she had to follow her heart toward Fitzwilliam and away from Quinn.

- - • -🔆- • - -

Would Bella need to die to save the fairy tales? She didn't want to dwell too long on that.

The conversation lulled, and Bella shut down her anxiety by focusing on lighter things. Gerard may have mocked her with his rude comments about books, but the words felt more like a brother's teasing than the former arrogant patron of The Swan in New Orleans. Somewhere during his new life Gerard had grown a heart, and Bella suspected it was aimed toward Aerowyn.

Bella yawned.

"Why don't you go back to the bedroom where you cleaned up and rest?" Aerowyn suggested. "You need the sleep."

"I think I will." Bella yawned again. "If you'll excuse me."

Back in her room tucked under soft covers, Bella drifted off to sleep on the cozy bed when Gerard's voice in her mind startled her awake.

*I'm going to try to convince Aerowyn to let me go with you on the ship to protect you, while she gets to the bottom of Peter's lies in the Kingdom of Magic.*

*You woke me up!*

*It doesn't matter. I need you to listen.*

Bella could well imagine his chest puffing out.

*Still acting like the arrogant war hero. What's so important that you needed to interrupt my sleep?*

Gerard continued, *Peter gave Callista magic when he changed her into a sea snake, so you're not going to be safe even in the air.*

Bella exhaled. *I think Captain Modo is supposed to protect me—not you. Besides, as a man, he can use his hands to fight her. You are limited to your paws.*

*You're so stubborn.*

*I could say the same about you.*

Gerard refused to accept her rejections when Bella first met him. He didn't like her, but he expected her full attention.

*It doesn't matter who is more stubborn. You can't underestimate Callista. Peter didn't curse her because of something she did, but rather something she didn't do.*

Bella glared at the wall as if she could glower at the wolf through a solid object. *And how do you know this?*

*Aerowyn has been sharing secrets with me. Callista is one of the villains who has ruined many of the fairy tales, which is Peter's fault, Callista didn't stop Isla from leaving the Kingdom of Magic and casting a spell that turned a princess into a dragon. I'm not sure why Peter expected Callista to stop his daughter when he couldn't, but she was Isla's friend.*

*How do a fae and mermaid become friends?* Bella wondered.

*I'm surprised you, the book-obsessed, didn't know that mermaids grow legs to replace their fins to be on land.*

Bella harrumphed. She sat up and placed her fists on her hips. *I did know that, toad, but book mermaids could be different from real ones.*

*You're grumpy. Go to sleep.*

Bella smiled. Some things would never change with Gerard, even when he was a wolf. Her grin faded. For some reason, it seemed that Peter needed her to fall in love with Fitzwilliam Modo, which must have been why Aerowyn insisted she had to be on the *Notre Dame,* and not another ship. A long sea journey should be the perfect romantic setting for true love to develop, but what if it didn't happen?

When she wished upon stars and dreamt of fairy tale love affairs with handsome princes, Bella could have imagined falling in love on a high-seas adventure, but those whimsical notions had lost some of their sheen. Harsh reality had disillusioned her.

Gerard interrupted her thoughts. *Don't lose your wishes upon stars for happily-ever-after.*

*You're breaking into my private thoughts again,* Bella scolded.

*I tease you about your bookish notions, but that's what makes you the person you are: entertaining, empathetic, and optimistic.* He huffed and lost some of his thoughtful tone. *That is also what will get us both out of this mess. I want to be a man again, and you want to return home. We need your crazy imagination to do that.*

Embarrassment flooded her that Gerard, of all people—or of all wolves—had read her mind. *I don't know if I should be mad at you for eavesdropping on my private thoughts or thank you for the kind words. You tell me to go to sleep, but then tell me you need my crazy imagination.* She heaved a sigh. *I will need to shut off my imagination if I'm to eventually fall asleep.*

Gerard said, *Tell yourself a story. Your tales always put me to sleep.*

A wolf can't laugh, but Bella almost thought she heard his thoughts guffaw.

She mentally recited one of the tales she had memorized, and eventually the long days of escaping enemies and living on borrowed time took their toll, and Bella fell asleep.

# Chapter 29

# Captain Modo

**M**odo peered through the white misty clouds from the fore-castle. He almost lost his footing when Aerowyn appeared suddenly out of nowhere, a great, black wolf on one side and Bella floating mid-air on the other.

Modo hobbled over to Bella, but his relief and elation turned to trepidation.

"Is she dead?"

"No, only sleeping with the aid of a strong spell." Aerowyn smiled slightly. "She's had a couple of long days." Then she looked the captain up and down. "It appears you have had some rough days as well. Let me fix that."

Aerowyn waved her gold scepter, and Modo's left leg muscles twitched, then quickly became pain-free. She swiped the scepter over his left ear, and his hearing returned.

"Now that I've taken care of that." She twirled the wand over Bella, and the girl disappeared. When Modo cried out, the enchantress added, "She's tucked into her bed. I only wanted you to know she's alive and once again in your care. I assumed you would find believing me easier if you saw her first."

The captain straightened. "Thank you."

Several crew members assembled hastily with weapons in hand. Growling, Gerard blocked the way to the enchantress.

"Stand down," Modo commanded. "Aerowyn and her wolf only came to deliver Bella."

"Aye, Captain," Westley replied.

"Is Beller alive?" Jeb asked, and Aerowyn nodded. "Wha' a relief!" Jeb exhaled while saying.

Gilbert pointed. "That's the woman! That's who Aerrol Flyntock turned into and—" he gulped, "Gregory Butler turned into the— the— wolf."

Aerowyn raised one eyebrow. "He won't harm you unless provoked. Now, has anyone seen Till?"

The slight, odd-looking, blond fellow with the jar of pixie dust appeared out of nowhere. "Did someone call my name?"

Modo began, "Where did you come—"

His words were cut off when Till transformed into a woman with wings.

"Captain Modo, this is Tilly, a pixie fairy from Ageless Isle. I asked her to accompany you in case the ship needed to become airborne. She knows what to do with a flying vessel."

The sailors gawked until Aerowyn warned, "She's too good for any of you, so please stop gaping at her."

All mouths snapped shut.

The wolf whined.

The enchantress looked at him.

After a few minutes she said, "Gerard wanted me to tell Captain Modo that Bella is special, and you shouldn't miss any more opportunities to tell her so."

Modo's face heated, and the men grinned while elbowing each other.

"Thank you for the unsolicited advice, Gerard." Modo said through clenched teeth.

Aerowyn smiled. In the blink of an eye, both she and Gerard vanished. The sailors stared wide-eyed.

Modo sighed. This wasn't going the way he thought it would.

# Chapter 30

# Aerowyn

Aerowyn entered the Kingdom of Magic with trepidation. Not wishing to appear out of thin air and provoke the fae, she and Gerard materialized under thick foliage in the dark forest that bordered the kingdom. Gerard's nostrils twitched as he sniffed rapidly.

Aerowyn, too, drew in a deep breath. She hadn't set foot in the kingdom since her father, the king of the fae, moved the fae to Ageless Isle, and the scents of exotic flowers and rich soil brought back both happy and mournful memories. Her father had transformed parts of the magic island to replicate her homeland, but Ageless Isle had never become her home.

When Peter had manipulated the fae to move to the isle, citing the threat of dragons in the realm near to their kingdom, they tried to make their new homes identical to the ones they had left. After the fae stopped following Peter blindly and returned to their former residence, all stayed the same. Each tree house's foliage shimmered in jeweled tones.

Nervous energy buzzed in Aerowyn's chest, and Gerard must have sensed it, for he nuzzled her hand.

She rested her fingertips on his head, drawing comfort from his presence. "I don't know if anyone will accept me here. I wasn't demanding like my father, but I didn't leave him when my best friend, Brynn, begged me to return."

*Brynn?*

"I never told you about her, but she got me through the death of my mother and sister."

*Why did she want you to come back here?*

"She tried to tell me my father was corrupt, but I didn't believe her. I love Father. It is hard to see the flaws in those you love."

*I'm sure she understood.*

"She was angry and hurt, and I don't blame her. Father has been cruel in his leadership, but so much time has passed that I don't know what to expect."

Gerard leaned against her leg. *You were being loyal to the only family you had left, even if he was wrong.*

Aerowyn shook her head. "Brynn's whole family was incinerated by dragon fire, and she was all alone except for Aidan, the fae who wanted to marry her. Long ages past, we didn't always marry, but humans' ways had already started to seep into our culture by then."

*She's probably forgiven you and is happily married.*

She squared her shoulders. "I hope so, that's why I'm going to her house first. I will have to change my appearance for her to recognize me." Aerowyn pulled her golden scepter with the jeweled sun-shaped tip out of thin air and glanced down at him. "You will finally get to see what I look like when I'm not disguising myself."

Aerowyn brushed the wand over her body, lifting the dulling spell which made her more human in appearance. Her skin turned a glittering porcelain, and her hair and eyes became more vivid.

Gerard studied her carefully. *You look the same, but more celestial. The rings of color in your eyes are different. It's a bit off-putting. I won't be able to read your mood.*

"It's hard to blend in around people without a little dulling spell. Some people cower in fear when we show them our true selves, so we stopped doing that centuries ago."

He cocked his wolfish head to the side. *How old are you?*

"That's not important. Let's find Brynn."

Gerard blew air through his nose in the dissatisfied way he always did when she wouldn't answer his questions. It almost made her smile.

They walked toward the intricate homes built into the gigantic, magical trees and their unnaturally colored foliage. Each house was slightly different from the next, matching the variations of jewel tones in the trees. Aerowyn approached the home with a pumpkin-colored roof at the edge of the village.

She held her breath and knocked on the orange door.

It opened, and the same Brynn stood before her, open mouthed. "Aerowyn," she said tentatively, "is that you?"

The enchantress whispered, "Yes."

Brynn's lips curled upward into a smile, and she pulled Aerowyn into a hug. "My dearest friend. I didn't think I would ever see you again."

"I didn't think so either." Tears welled up in Aerowyn's eyes, but before she could doubt herself, she said, "I need your help to defeat Father."

Brynn's musical laugh immediately put Aerowyn at ease. "I see you haven't changed. We haven't spoken for centuries, and you get right to the reason for your visit rather than attempt any small talk." She smiled down at Gerard. "Could you at least introduce me to this handsome wolf? After all, a man you cursed but who still accompanies you and is ready to jump to your defense requires an introduction."

*How does she know that?*

"This is Gerard," Aerowyn said, "and he is curious how you know he is a man."

Brynn smiled at him. "Wolves don't like our scent or glittering skin. We scare them, and they stay away from us. Aerowyn either cursed a man or made a wolf into a pet. Besides, Gerard, your eyes definitely look human."

"As much as I would love to talk for hours about our separate lives, I need your help. I fear Father and my spells have finally gone past the point of no return."

Her oldest friend grew serious and stepped aside to usher them in. "Come in, then, and have some tea. Aidan, my husband will be happy to see you."

It felt homey. Like Aerowyn's abode on Ageless Isle, plants grew from the inner walls, and the green herbal sides of the sitting room produced a minty, lemon verbena scent.

Brynn sat on a blue corn-flower-shaped chaise and directed Aerowyn to sit on a white rose-shaped chair. Gerard sat next to her and sniffed wildly. He finally settled down as his senses grew accustomed to all the aromas.

Brynn called out, "Aiden, we have guests."

Aidan, the same white-blond fae Aerowyn remembered, emerged from the adjacent kitchen.

"Aer, is that you?"

"Yes. I need your—"

He hugged her, muffling her words in his embrace.

"She needs our help," Brynn finished for her.

Aidan released Aerowyn and turned toward his wife.

"Would you be a dear," she asked, "and get us some tea? It's going to be a tough conversation."

"Then I'll make it a strong tea." Aidan's dimpled smile flashed at Brynn, and he returned to the kitchen.

An awkward silence descended while the three of them waited, but Aidan soon returned with a pot of green-colored tea.

Aerowyn accepted a delicate cup and began, "I recently learned that my father has been lying to me about several things."

Gerard nudged her knee, and she set a hand on his head.

Brynn took a sip from her cup. "Yes, he has."

"Do you know about..." She sighed. "All his lies?"

"It took years to discover all of them." Brynn glanced at Aidan.

Aerowyn exhaled her next words. "Please tell me what you have discovered." She removed her palm from Gerard's head and used both hands to cradle the teacup.

Aidan groaned. "Where do we start?"

"What was the first lie you unraveled once you left Ageless Isle?" Aerowyn covered her anxiety by taking a sip.

"Well, there were the lies about the pendants King Peter made us wear." Brynn's lips pursed. "He said they gave us powers and immortality, then demanded we surrender them when we left the isle. Yet, we were able to return to the Kingdom of Magic in seconds using magic." Brynn sat up straight. "You can see we haven't aged, so the charms didn't give us immortality either."

"I learned about that falsehood after a sea fight with Callista. She tore it off me in an effort to kill me."

Brynn gasped. "That's horrible! I didn't realize that witch was still terrorizing the seas."

Gerard whined, and Aerowyn whispered, "I know. You hated that day."

The couple exchanged a look Aerowyn couldn't decipher.

Brynn studied her beverage. "What else have you learned?"

"Father created the first dragon. He wanted to end his life after Mother died, and he thought the creature would destroy us. He eventually came to his senses and wanted to continue living, but it was too late. He moved us to Ageless Isle to cover up his mistake."

Gerard growled.

Aidan echoed Gerard's anger as he exclaimed, "That's vile."

Aerowyn nodded solemnly. "Yes, it is. My father created a beast to kill his people, all to hide from his own pain."

"Actually..." Aidan leaned back in his chair. "Dragons don't kill us. That was either an error on Peter's part or another lie."

"Aidan!" Brynn eyed her husband crossly. "I'm sorry, my friend. He shouldn't have thrown that on you so abruptly."

"No, I need to hear the truth." Aerowyn frowned. "Bella, the girl who Father maintains will fix his mess, said dragon fire doesn't kill us, but the information came from one of my father's victims. I didn't know if I could believe her. Does that mean my sister is alive?"

"Yes—" Aidan cast a glance at Brynn who nodded "—but before you go looking for her or feeling hurt that she has never contacted you, you need to know that Isla is no longer fae."

For a second, Aerowyn stopped breathing. Gerard nosed her arm.

She swallowed. "What do you mean?"

Brynn reached out and took Aerowyn's hand. "She remained a dragon. Once she was incinerated, she was reborn into a dragon, much the way a phoenix burns up and then rises from the cinders."

Aerowyn's mouth gaped. "Isla is a dragon?"

"Yes." Brynn set her cup onto a smoothed tree stump. "She used to have the ability to speak, but that faded to only telepathic communication. Now..." She shook her head. "After so many years of being in a reptile's body, Isla lost herself. She is but a ferocious dragon and has created an army from the fae who we thought died in battle against the dragons."

Aidan set down his cup by Brynn's. "We spend most our days trying to protect all the people who live in Terradraco from the consequences of your father's acts."

"For their sakes, ours, and our daughter's." Brynn's hand moved to her stomach.

Diverted and genuinely surprised, Aerowyn repeated, "Daughter?"

"Yes." A small, happy smile pulled at Brynn's lips.

Questions ran through Aerowyn's mind—How old was she? What was her name? Could she meet her?—All she managed to say was, "But Father said we could not..."

Anger stopped her. It had been another lie. Though he had taken a human wife, her father had forbidden associating with humans, even though he declared it was the only way to bear children. Now that Aerowyn knew it was his fault the dragons existed, it made sense that he wanted to keep the fae far from his mistake.

She drew a deep breath and said, "I would very much like to meet her."

"That might be difficult at the moment." Brynn grinned from ear to ear and placed her hand over her stomach. "She's brewing up her own magic in here."

Aerowyn stared intensely at Brynn's middle. The flowing gown masked her friend's pregnancy.

Aidan laughed heartily. "You can't see her yet, Aer."

Brynn grinned. "We can feel her emotions. Like all babies, she won't figure out language until she is older, but for now, I can treasure having her all to myself." She winked at her husband. "I'll share with him later."

Aidan's quick grin faded. "For now, though, how can we help? Do you truly plan on thwarting King Peter?"

"I must." Aerowyn dropped her head. "Somewhere along the line Father appointed himself judge and jury."

Gerard nudged his head against her leg. *It'll be all right.*

"I hope so," she whispered so that only he heard.

Aerowyn's worst fear was those hexed would never be free from their curses. More misery would be in the world than before they started the quest to rid it of selfishness. In fact, with creatures like Callista, bitterness would replace selfishness or make it worse.

"Aer, it wasn't only King Peter's tyranny that changed our ways. We have been interacting—even intermingling—with humans for a long time. We now uphold standards of propriety and have adopted their ideas of marriage and family.

*Have you ever wanted to marry?*

The wolf's question brought her to a stop. She bit her lip rather than reveal to him that she had. But that was irrelevant when the hexes and curses threw the world into chaos. Keeping her eyes on her childhood friend, she said, "Thank you, but all that you've told me isn't ultimately the information I need. I must look through our ancient manuscripts and see if the curses Father and I have cast can be reversed. We invoke the hexes and say only unselfish acts or changed behavior could break them, but Gerard here is an example of that not being the perfect fix."

He froze at her side. *Do you mean that?*

She gave him a small smile. "Yes."

Brynn looked from Aerowyn to Gerard, a tiny frown on her face. "So how do you intend to remedy that?"

"The fairy tales of our kind that have been shared in the human realm have become twisted. Our stories are no longer appearing the way they were originally written. Father believes Bellarose—"

"Is that the human girl you mentioned?"

Aerowyn nodded. "Bella can reverse all the damage he's done if she has her happy ending, but how can that be?"

"I never understood how our history became entertaining story books for the humans," Aidan commented.

Aerowyn sighed. "I don't either."

"My mother told me long ago that whenever our people wanted to record our histories, they kidnapped scholars from the human realm to record the accounts," Brynn explained. "It was too tedious a task for the fae because they couldn't use magic to make quick work of it."

"Why couldn't they use magic?" Aerowyn asked.

"Mother said the magic that the fae used for creating books somehow caused the history documented to repeat itself in a never-ending loop. They burned the first book once they realized they were living the same days over and over again."

Aerowyn tapped her finger on her teacup. "So could the human scholars have written our histories in their own books and claimed they were fictional?"

*That's what I was wondering.*

"Yes, because after the fae borrowed people to write our histories, they made them forget it ever happened, but the stories stayed planted in their subconscious. They wrote them down as fairy tales for their children to enjoy." Brynn frowned.

Aidan asked, "Why the grumpy face my love?"

"I think the way our ancestors treated humans was horrible. I'm glad we are now allied with them instead. We can commission them to write our records rather than enslaving them."

"I don't know how it is possible, but Father says the stories changed, as if we have lived all of this before but with different endings."

Brynn absentmindedly rubbed her belly. "My mother said that the ancient fae could travel through dimensions and see futures and pasts. Our people haven't repeated history since my mother was born. King Peter probably went to another time to see what the stories were or should have been."

"Do any of the fae time travel?" Aerowyn's mouth turned downward. "I knew nothing about it until Father confessed that he did it."

"No." Brynn sighed. "The fae no longer traverse through time. Once your father became king, he made our elders swear an oath to not use dimension travel. He thought it was too dangerous. We lost our ability when the elders cast the binding spell to make the promise permanent."

Aerowyn's thoughts exploded at the realization of her father's motives.

Aidan must have come to the same conclusion. "Brynn, you realize why King Peter stopped time travel, don't you?"

"Yes, I believe we all figured it out."

Tears gathered in Aerowyn's eyes. "My Father didn't want anyone to see the consequences of what he had done by creating the dragons. He killed off his own people."

"Aer, it isn't hopeless. We can't undo what we've lost, but we can fix things."

Aerowyn's eyes streamed, and her nose dripped. "How?"

Aidan silently stood up and crossed the room to hand Aerowyn a handkerchief.

Brynn put an arm around Aerowyn, and Gerard leaned into her opposite leg.

"Well," Brynn said bracingly, "now that we know what has happened to the stories, we can figure out how to break all the hexes. I'm sure our histories have the answers."

"You're right of course," Aerowyn sniffed as she wiped her nose. "But I've had to turn off all my emotions except for the ones that elevated justice and anger. I never even cried for Isla. Father shamed me into helping him rid the world of what he had claimed was selfishness, but... haven't our actions been selfish too?"

"Oh, Aer," Brynn murmured.

Aerowyn's sobs resumed. "Some of the curses worked, and some rather despicable aristocrats changed into kind and generous people. Gerard, however, sacrificed his humanity for his brother to break his curse and he remained a wolf." She raised teary eyes to the wolf at her side, but there was no judgement in his expression. "That made me think not all our enchantments were purely for vindication of the weak and poor, but more to help rid Father of guilt."

Aidan handed her another handkerchief. "And once you cast a spell, you can't reverse it. But isn't there always a way to break it?"

"Yes, but Father had me use the curses that require true sacrifice to end them, so someone always must give up their life or humanity. I thought the punishment wasn't supposed to be permanent." She clenched her hands around the damp cloth. "Gerard shouldn't have to be a wolf forever. He has proven to me he is no longer selfish or arrogant."

The wolf whined.

"I know, Gerard. You *should* have your happily-ever-after. I thought, after all you've done to help me, you would wake up one morning a man, and it hasn't happened yet." She wiped her cheeks and dropped to the floor to look him in the eye. "I want you to be a man more than you know."

He refused to answer, and her heart hurt. Aerowyn knew he didn't regret helping his brother and that he understood the pain of loss. Aerowyn had given him false hope, and the recognition of that fact hurt her.

"Right!" Aidan interrupted the intense stare between Gerard and Aerowyn. "Then it's time to look for some answers! I'm going to our archives to search. Anyone want to come?"

He opened the front door. Brynn went outside first, and Gerard followed.

"I'm sorry," Aerowyn whispered to the empty cottage.

She pushed herself to her feet and followed them all.

What if the solutions she sought didn't exist? Would she live forever isolated and unloved like those she bewitched? Could she find forgiveness and a joyful ending?

It was a dream magic couldn't fulfil, but even enchantresses have wishes.

# Chapter 31

# Gerard

The fae archive was a never-ending warehouse of tomes. Designed to keep out light, moisture, and other elements that would damage the ancient manuscripts, the room's stained-glass windows were, in fact, artificial. The whole place with its magical books made Gerard's hackles rise.

Yet every day, he accompanied Aerowyn and her friends to the archives. Pine, cloves, oranges, paper, leather, ink, and occasional hints of sulfur invaded Gerard's sensitive nose. He asked Aerowyn about it on the first day, and she told him that she suspected it was part of the magic used to keep the manuscripts from deteriorating, though he never saw evidence of her theory.

When he first padded onto the marble floors, the cool, smooth surface was a little unnerving since he was accustomed to more rustic material. The shelves of books reminded him of the library Aerowyn installed on *Notre Dame* for Bella. He allowed himself a wolfish smile when he imagined the girl's reaction to this room.

Thinking of Bella made his mind flurry. What if, after everything they'd done to protect Bella, the witch or dragon find a way to hurt her? Would they ruin Aerowyn's chance to repair things? What if Peter discovered that Aerowyn was trying to thwart his plans? Would she be in danger? Gerard hated being helpless.

The three fae read for days, pouring over any book that might contain the answers they sought. And every day, Gerard paced, nails clicking on the floor. He wasn't content retrieving buckets of water for drinking water. He wanted to do more. Gerard's muscles twitched with anxious energy. The room was too confining to stretch and release tension.

He whined.

Aerowyn reprimanded him. *Please settle down. You're very distracting and reading the ancient language requires concentration.*

*I need to do something.* He grunted. *I have experience fighting, strategizing, and whatever is needed.*

Aerowyn frowned. *Unfortunately, we need supernatural powers, and you can't help with that.* She rubbed behind his ear, which normally calmed him, but this time it didn't.

Tail swishing, Gerard ran into the forest to burn off his twitchiness. He sniffed every new scent along the way but continued running. When his restlessness subsided, he returned to the archive building. The structure's columns reminded him of a miniature plantation and his brother Antoine. Gerard missed him, but his desire to see Aerowyn safe overpowered the longing to be with his family again.

With his edginess gone, Gerard trotted back inside and collapsed panting on the plush cushion there for his use. Aerowyn was reading what must have been the thousandth book—an old manuscript written centuries before—when she suddenly exclaimed, "I found the answer we seek!"

Gerard perked up from the corner. Aidan and Brynn's droopy eyes widened.

"What is it?" Brynn's voice grew perkier with relief.

"It requires only me, and if I share, then it won't work." She stared across the room. "I will need to go back to the mortal realm, and all should be as it was before Father, and I broke the fairy tales."

*You're speaking in riddles. What does that mean, Aerowyn?* Gerard strained to read her thoughts.

She didn't answer.

"Aer, you know I will read that manuscript as soon as you leave." Aidan's typically mischievous smile seemed dimmer. "I'm as curious as a cat."

"That's why I will be taking this page with me."

To Gerard's surprise and the fae's gasps of horror, Aerowyn tore the page from the book.

"Oh, don't worry. If I can, I'll put it back once I'm done, in case another fae gets caught in the same twisted magic in the future."

Gerard only heard an echo of her thoughts.

He bit back a growl. *What do you mean, if you can?*

She met his eyes, then looked away and swallowed visibly. After she tucked the paper into her pocket, she said aloud, "You must trust me. You won't remember I found the solution."

"What's that supposed to mean?" Brynn looked skeptical.

Instead of explaining, Aerowyn embraced her friends. She reached a hand to Gerard. "We need to leave. At once."

He trotted over to her side, and she placed a trembling hand on his head.

"Goodbye," she said. Sights, sounds, and smells assaulted Gerard's senses as she misted them away from the Kingdom of Magic.

# Chapter 32

# Bellarose

B ella awoke refreshed. She stretched and eased stiffly out of bed. Immediately, her nightgown dissolved, and the mystical room pulled a sensible dress over her head, brushed her hair, and tied it back in a matching ribbon. When everything seemed to be in its place—and she thought she looked pretty enough to meet her destiny—she proceeded to leave the room when...

"Ahoy, Cap'n," sounded loudly outside her door as the room tipped slightly.

Startled by the male voice and the motion, Bella knew she wasn't on Ageless Isle anymore. Aerowyn had tricked her with two identical rooms. The enchantress must have returned Bella to the *Notre Dame* during her slumber.

Adjusting mentally to her current location, she squared her shoulders and went to meet her future.

Modo was on the main deck, as she suspected he would be. Before he noticed she was there, the thought of that perfect kiss came to mind. Would he be the same man he was when they were held captive? Would he ignore her again? She bit her bottom lip, but when his eyes met hers, his words washed away her fear.

"Bella, you're awake! Aerowyn brought you back to us with strict instructions to stay in the clouds."

Astonished, Bella looked to starboard. The *Notre Dame* wasn't rocking upon the ocean but rather fluffy, white cottony puffs that billowed around them. She gasped.

"Is Gerard here too? He said he wanted to join us."

Modo's brows knitted together. "How could the wolf tell you that?"

"He talked to my mind."

He shook his head. "I would ask how a wolf can communicate with your mind, but nothing is strange when it involves the enchantress and her curses. No, he's with Aerowyn. Anyway, we're bound for New Orleans."

"Your leg and your ear?" she exclaimed. "Are you well? I was worried you would be injured all over again when I pushed you off Eira's back into that net."

Modo gave her a huge grin. "Both are good as new. Aerowyn healed them. I guess some magic doesn't come with a hefty price. I'm injury free without having to sell my soul or be turned into a beast."

Bella giggled. "I'm happy to hear that."

He motioned for her to accompany him to the forecastle.

"You know," she said, "flying on Eira's back, the air was thin and cold, but this isn't. Who is making the air comfortable for us?"

"Tilly, the pixie fairy, came along to help us fly with her dust and special abilities." He motioned for Bella to sit on the bench. "At first, she disguised herself as one of my crew, but when Aerowyn dropped you off, Tilly's true identity was revealed." He turned to face her, kindness in his brown eyes. "How are you?"

Modo's gentle expression gave Bella hope that his attitude toward her hadn't changed at all. The worry lifted and she felt as light as a cloud.

"I'm well," she said shyly. "I think. I don't want to be too confident since things never go as expected. Who knows, Aerowyn could have changed a prince into an evil nebula ready to pounce on the ship as we speak."

Modo chuckled. It seemed out-of-character, but maybe it wasn't and his smile warmed Bella to her toes. "I think we're safe from evil clouds, but in case I'm wrong, I have my sword handy." Then he winked at Bella.

Butterflies fluttered in her stomach. "What happened to the no nonsense Captain Modo?"

"Whatever do you mean?"

"You smiled, winked, and laughed all within a minute of each other."

"Have you forgotten what I told you on the island?" Modo asked softly.

Tingles went down her back. "Which part?"

"If there weren't so many eyes watching us, I would at least show you part of the conversation with my lips." Modo's face turned red, contradicting his bold confession.

That blush only endeared him even more to her. She placed her palm on his.

He continued, "I didn't want our separation to be permanent, and I'm so thankful it wasn't. We have a long journey ahead of us, and I want to take advantage of this second—or maybe it's a third—chance. I've lost count of how many times I bungled our encounters, but when I thought you could die, that rattled me. I'm more concerned with you than with propriety."

Bella swallowed hard. "Captain Modo, you have stunned me speechless. I don't know what to say."

"Say you will dine with me and my officers this evening? Then you and I will watch the stars in this very spot."

"Yes," was all Bella could manage.

He smiled. "Good. I must return to my duties." He stood and took a few steps before he turned and grinned. "Also, please just call me Fitz."

She didn't swoon, but she felt like she could. It seemed the debonair captain had developed the skills to sweep her off her feet like one of the princes in her fairy tales.

· · ● ·  ☀  · ● · ·

Finn brought the food into the officer's dining area. He blushed seeing Bella.

"Cap'n." He shifted his weight. "May I speak to Bella?"

Modo nodded. "Of course."

"I was awful worried about you. You don't have to marry me. I'm thankful you're alive." His gaze fell as he rocked back and forth on his feet. "I made you apple pie as an offerin' to let you know we're still friends."

Bella smiled. "Thank you, Finn. I'm honored to be your friend and will savor every bite of that pie."

The cook beamed. "That means the world to me."

Finn finished delivering all the food and exited.

The food Finn had prepared for the officers, the captain, and her was probably delectable, but Bella couldn't focus on the flavors. Her mind was whirling at the new Modo—the one she was now to think of as Fitz, which didn't suit him either. Something about his mannerisms was familiar, but it was never similar enough to bring up the person he emulated.

Dinner conversation was casual. With Westley, a couple of officers and Jeb present, there weren't any declarations like the ones he had made quietly to her earlier. Sometimes Jeb would say something to make her laugh, but her attention wasn't completely on her old friend's words. She was fixated on Captain Modo—his smile, his eyes, his lips.

"Beller."

She startled and turned.

Jeb was looking right at her.

"Did you 'ear me?"

"Oh, I'm sorry, Jeb. I didn't. My mind has been wandering all night. I guess this adventure gives me plenty to ponder."

"I asked if ya were scared ridin' that dragon?"

Bella clutched her chest. "I was terrified! I know we're flying as we speak, but it feels different with boards and rails to steady you. I had only her scales to hold onto and some weak vines tied around me."

The men laughed at her honesty, and Modo's huge grin made her stomach flip.

"I was a little intimidated, myself," Modo piped in. "I had the advantage—or maybe disadvantage—of playing dead, but keeping my eyes closed helped tremendously."

"You still had to hold on without showing Eira that you were alive because those vines wouldn't have held a tiny child and I didn't trust her magic abilities to secure us while she flew. We certainly had to be creative."

"Yes, we did." He winked, and she felt giddy.

A scullion took her plate and the empty serving dishes. Bella must have enjoyed the meal, but she couldn't recall one morsel that touched her tongue. She was glad Finn was busy elsewhere because he always asked for her approval on his creations. She didn't want to lie but would have to because of the crazy thoughts flipping through her mind.

"Bella, the clouds have disappeared, and the sky is full of stars." Modo held out his hand to help her from of her chair. "Would you like to join me under them?"

The crew at the table smirked, nudged each other in the sides, but said nothing.

"Yes, that sounds delightful."

When she stood, the men also arose, and she placed her arm in the crook of Modo's and allowed him to escort her out of the room. The suppressed chuckles from the men made her feel like a spectacle.

She kept her eyes down. They knew Modo was courting her and must have guessed she was attracted to him.

She wasn't in love with Modo, but how could she fall in love under the watchful eyes of so many? It should be a private thing between them.

"I'm sorry about that," he said quietly, interrupting her racing thoughts. "I didn't think asking you to view some stars would evoke such a reaction. I will talk with them tomorrow."

"Thank you, but perhaps it isn't necessary."

They reached the forecastle. Ensuring none were nearby to eavesdrop, Modo turned Bella to face him. "I don't want whatever this is to be viewed by all as if we were on stage," he told her gently. "I'll talk to them."

"She gazed up at him. "Thank you."

Modo leaned in for a kiss. His lips touched hers, both soft and intense. It was mind-blowing, unequivocal bliss.

When they fell apart, Bella took in air, but before she could kiss him again, he straightened and touched her cheek.

"I think I'm getting the hang of this, but I hope I'm not being too forward."

"I did kiss you first." Bella glanced down. "I've never been that brazen with any man, and I felt ashamed afterwards. Again, maybe I've been around pirates for too long. Before I know it, I'll start swearing like a sailor."

Modo laughed. "I doubt that, but I can bring out my highly austere Captain Modo performance again if you need reminding how a proper lady should act."

She raised her eyebrows. "Was that a performance? I never could tell. But, during one of your more pleasant moments, I temporarily lost my sanity and kissed you."

"As long as you are now completely of sound mind, I don't care about who kissed whom first. And yes, it was an act." He hesitated. "I'm not from an elite, highly sophisticated family. I don't know how to act a proper gentleman, but I didn't want to be mistaken for a scoundrel. When it comes to you, Bella, I want to be the best man I can be."

It was the most extraordinary thing a man had ever said to her, and her heart overflowed.

At that moment, she wanted nothing more than to love Modo, but somewhere deep inside, common sense whispered that to get her happy ending, there had to be more than a storybook version of rushing into love. Her true joy would be with a man who was more than a gorgeous face and a great kisser. She wanted to know what made him tick and wanted to love him even after discovering his flaws. Her parents didn't have that kind of love, and she wanted something more than they'd had.

She studied his handsome face. "We're both new at this. I never kissed a man before you, though some tried. I feel honored that you want to be your best with me and can only hope I am deserving of such a commitment." She looked up at the stars. "I do want to be clear that kissing doesn't mean falling in love. I want to get to know you better. I hope that during this journey we will be able to."

"I agree. I'm sorry I kept you at a distance." He fell quiet, then added, "I told you the truth. I've never kissed a woman before you."

"That really surprises me, because handsome men like you usually get lots of experience especially on shore leave."

That grin spread across his face again. "Are you saying I'm handsome?"

Bella turned away to avoid his scrutiny. "Yes, but you did say I was the most beautiful woman you have ever seen."

"I meant it. I didn't say it for you to return the favor."

"That's not what I meant. I- I meant- I was saying I felt-"

"Bella," he said softly. "It's all right."

She sighed. "Based on our previously awkward encounters, we may have challenges getting to know each other."

"I was afraid to show you the real me. I have secrets I'm supposed to keep that I was afraid to reveal if we got too close."

"What kind of secrets?" Bella's eyes narrowed. In her experience, secrets protected misconduct.

"Aerowyn's secrets."

"Oh," she said disbelievingly, "Not something like you're married or are transformed from a horse?"

Modo laughed out loud. "No, nothing like that. I did hear you tell Jeb I could be enchanted from an animal, but I assure you I'm one hundred percent man and I've never been married."

Bella covered her eyes with her palms. "Oh no! You did hear our conversation. I'm sorry my imagination got the better of me that day."

"No, I understand." He gave her a warm smile. "Dealing with Aerowyn's hexes and reading a lot of fairy tales, can make one jump to hasty conclusions."

"I'm thankful you are an unmarried man, but secrets are usually bad." She sighed. "I'm still a little skeptical since it involves Aerowyn. I don't want the enchantress or her curses to influence our feelings toward each other."

"I agree. Wherever our relationship takes us. It needs to be real and not conjured up for some fae's personal end. If we're supposed to fall in love, it must be on our own terms or not at all."

"I'm bursting from curiosity." Bella fidgeted with her hair then blurted, "Do you know Aerowyn's scheme for us?"

"Do you mean what Aerowyn has planned for each of us individually?" Modo met her eyes.

"No, for us as a couple." Bella's face was on fire. "Aerowyn and her father want us to fall in love."

Modo pulled at his collar. "Is that what Aerowyn told you?"

"Aerowyn didn't exactly use those words, but I guessed. She told me why I've been forced into so many perilous situations."

"She put your life in danger on purpose?" His voice tightened.

"No. The danger came from her mistakes, or rather from the creatures she cursed." Bella bit her bottom lip. "She told me that if I have a happy ending, maybe I will reverse their errors."

Modo raked his fingers through his hair. "How are you going to undo magic when you have none of your own?"

"Supposedly, if my wishes come true, all will be well. It seems that the stories in my books are real, and have been twisted from all the hexed creatures seeking revenge. With my imagination and knowledge of how the stories should end, Peter thinks I'm the key to the solution."

Modo exhaled sharply. "That is far-fetched."

"That's what I said. Peter didn't really explain to Aerowyn how it works, and he's lied to her in the past. She's visiting her people who live in the Kingdom of Magic to ask them because they know more about the ancient curses and spells."

Modo paled, and a scowl made a deep crease between his eyebrows.

Bella touched his arm. "What's wrong? You look like you either saw a ghost or are about to be sick."

"Tell me"—Modo's voice faltered—"does 'happy ending' mean you must die happy?"

Hot tears welled in her eyes. "We all have to die eventually, but yes, I hope I will be happy."

"I understand that, but that isn't what I meant, Bella." Pain was etched on his face. "I'm asking if you have to die soon to fix these tales?"

"I... honestly, I wondered the same thing." She wrapped her arms around her waist. "I'm not ready to die yet. Aerowyn said it is a possibility, but it could also mean I end up with all my dreams coming true and am able to rewrite the tales on paper like an author would."

"I'm not ready for you to die either. I want more of what we're doing now. Talking. Being friends." His expression softened. "What we did earlier would be nice to repeat too."

The conversation lulled as they watched the diamond studded night sky. It was romantic beyond anything Bella had ever read about in her books or could have conjured up in her imagination. When they did speak, the chat turned away from their uncertain futures and toward a casual discussion of likes and dislikes. Based on his questions and comments, Modo knew Bella better than she knew him. Had he always been paying attention to her, even when she hadn't noticed?

Despite the sparkly blackened sky and a glowing moon enhancing the ambience, and her contentment, Bella yawned.

Modo smiled. "I think you should get some sleep. We can talk tomorrow. I can't promise it will be as private as it has been tonight, but I enjoy any time spent with you."

"I am rather tired." She yawned again. "Tonight, has been magical, but seeing each other in the light of day will give us another perspective. In this setting, my mind keeps straying to kissing you. Maybe if we're surrounded by the crew, it will force me to focus on your other attributes. I mean—" She held her palms to her suddenly blazing cheeks. "—It's not that all I think about when we're alone is kissing, but, well, being around others will allow me to see more than your lips." Bella covered her eyes with her hands. "I can't believe I just said that."

Modo's low laugh rumbled. "I think I know what you mean."

Bella's insides burned from embarrassment.

"What I'm trying to say is that I can't fall in love with someone I don't know, even if I love the way he kisses."

Modo remained quiet for several seconds, before saying, "I can't deny the thought of you wanting to kiss again brings me great pleasure, but I confess that I've observed you more than you have me, which has given me enough information to form opinions without a romantic setting."

She peeked through her fingers. "Is that good or bad?"

"Most definitely good."

"Are you going to expound on that?"

"Not now." He tucked her hand through his arm again. "Come on. It's late. I'll walk you back."

Bella's emotions whirled with possibilities during the short walk back to her cabin. Modo opened the door and ushered her in, then pressed a quick kiss on her lips before pulling the door shut and leaving Bella alone with her thoughts.

· ◦ ● ⟶☀⟵ ● ◦ ·

Despite the surplus of excitement, Bella fell asleep quickly, but her dreams were unsettling. She would be in the middle of a romantic kiss with Modo, when Quinn, her lost love, would appear. He didn't look angry or hurt when he saw her betray him, but rather pleased. Pain that she had rejected Quinn made dream-Bella push Modo away.

When she woke up, the twittering feelings Modo had evoked the previous night with his words and kisses had dulled. She blamed it on night visions of Quinn, but deep down, she worried the fabulous moonlit backdrop had confused her true feelings. She needed to forget Quinn once and for all. She could avoid him when she returned to New Orleans because he kept to the stables to avoid prying eyes.

But what if any feelings between her and Modo weren't strong enough for him to change careers? Would he be content to settle on land and give up the ocean? She gave herself a shake. They would cross that bridge when it was needed.

Bella exited her room to search for Modo, but he was there waiting for her.

She smiled widely. "Were you standing there all night, or do you have good timing?"

"I have good timing. I was about to knock to see if you were ready for breakfast, so I could join you. I don't believe we have ever eaten the morning meal together."

"That would be nice." She couldn't help adding, "We haven't because you were great at avoiding me most days."

Modo frowned. "I truly regret that. I guess our near-death experience had its benefits."

"What kind of benefits? I can only think of one." Bella's lips curled upward.

His frown dissolved into a smile. "It revealed to me that losing you would be worse than exposing my insecurities to you."

"Then it was good that I dived in after you after Callista almost drowned you." Bella teased.

His lightened expression faded. "Bella, I never want you to risk your life for me again, even if it did work out last time."

"It was a crazy move on my part, but you have risked your life for me. I always pay my debts." His seriousness prompted her to tease, "Besides, if you recall, I must live for all the curses to break, or at least long enough to find happiness to end the spells. After that I have no idea what will happen."

All levity disappeared from his face. "Don't take risks, Bella. Aerowyn may not be able to stop your death. She's not everywhere." Modo grabbed her hands and looked into her eyes. "Please promise that you'll try to be careful."

"I promise."

A secure warmth permeated Bella's inside.

Until she met Quinn, she never felt safe. When she was taken away from his protection, she was always on edge. There were short interludes where all seemed secure, but they were punctuated by villains attempting to kidnap or manipulate her.

But now... She felt safe on the *Notre Dame*, holding Modo's hands.

Bit by bit, the austere captain was edging into the prominent place Quinn had held in her heart.

Beyond doubt, Bella was falling for Captain Modo.

# Chapter 33

# Captain Modo

M odo loved Bella.

True, he'd had doubts about his feelings before now. Between all their misunderstandings and his arrogance, insecurities, and fears, he didn't know what was real until he spent time with her. She was the same Bella his old self, Quinn, had loved.

The doubts he once had over her only liking his handsome features were gone. She wasn't in love with the way he looked, although he was able to make her blush so easily with his newfound confidence. At first, he attributed his self-assurance to his appearance, but once they kissed, he felt invincible. She was all he would ever want or need until the end of time.

He pulled his attention back to the present. As they ate their morning porridge, Bella repeated the tales that were warped by Peter's tyranny.

"Once I started to recall my childhood stories, I began to remember how they were supposed to go. I would bet that if I search my library on this ship for fairy tales, they will be replaced with the new twisted ones."

"How could they change?" He took a sip of tea and frowned. "I imagine there are several tomes all around the world. Were they written in magical ink that can be erased and replaced?"

"I have no idea. Please don't think I'm daft, but sometimes I think I came from another era and don't belong here at all."

"You mean like you traveled in time?"

"Yes, exactly."

His lips quirked. "That's impossible."

"Really? Dragons and mermaids exist so why not time travel?"

He conceded her point, but uneasiness crept in at the thought. If Bella belonged in a different time, would she have to return? If she fell in love with him and broke all the spells, would she immediately exit this world and forget him? Would he forget her or be broken-hearted forever? No, he could never forget Bella.

"I'm not saying I know that for sure," she was saying. "I've had so many unusual experiences since Aerowyn started manipulating my life that my imagination confuses dreams and fairy tales with reality."

"Would it be selfish to admit that I hope you're wrong? I don't want you to leave."

Two thin lines formed between Bella's eyebrows and from experience he knew she was concentrating.

"I don't want to leave you, but say we fall in love. Then what?"

"What do you mean?"

"Will you come to live in New Orleans or expect me to sail with you forever?"

Her question flummoxed him. Modo hadn't thought that far in advance. Life had thrown sour twists at him all the time. Someone once made a sweet drink out of lemons at his father's pub. While doing so may be a metaphor for turning the sour into something good, if there were too many lemons to squeeze before they spoiled, they would remain lemons—only they'd be rotten. He didn't have time to turn his life of lemons into something sweet before time ran out.

"It will be determined by what happens between us," he finally said.

"I see." Bella gave him a smile Modo knew well.

Modo's heart thumped wildly as he gazed into Bella's emerald eyes, but no. They were surrounded by sailors. He resolutely squashed the urge to kiss her again.

For the remainder of the day, Modo showed Bella different parts of the ship and any tasks she could learn. She insisted on working for her keep despite his claim that everything was provided by Aerowyn. Bella wanted to be useful. This endeared her to him even more. He had observed so many entitled people in his past life that her unselfish desires were refreshing.

After the mid-day meal, he offered to teach her more techniques with the sword.

It was great exercise, and all the skills Bella had learned back in the stables seemed to return. Before long, he forgot to worry about being Modo, not Quinn, and simply enjoyed the clash of metal on metal. It was Bella from the old times. Contentment settled in his heart.

At length, she called a halt. Breathing heavily, she gasped, "You know. This reminds me of someone else I used to swordplay with, back in Louisiana."

Without thinking he asked, "Who?"

Her shoulders drooped at his question. Her downcast face instantly informed him of his mistake.

A tear slid down her face. "I told you about him before—the man I thought I loved. He didn't love me back."

Modo's own heart pinched. She was broken-hearted, and it was his fault.

He didn't want her to mourn over Quinn. He *was* Quinn, after all, and he loved her still. He just couldn't tell her.

Instead, he pointed to a barrel for Bella to sit on and he scooped up a cup of water for her from the clean storage tank on deck.

"I'm sorry. I forgot about that. I didn't mean to bring up such a painful memory," he said. "We should take a break anyway."

Bella gazed at the clouds that tumbled past. Another tear tracked down her cheek. "I thought I was over him. Perhaps that's why I can't know for sure if I love you yet. I'm still thinking about him. Quinn is in New Orleans. When I return home, I will be able to avoid him since he mainly sticks to his father's stables." She exhaled heavily. "I had a terrible dream about him last night, and that stirred this all up."

Torn between concern for her feelings and curiosity, he only asked, "What kind of dream?"

Bella's face reddened.

"It's embarrassing to say, but well"—she lowered her voice and glanced around—"you and I were kissing. When Quinn appeared, I felt like I was betraying him, but he acted like it didn't bother him at all. That hurt." She sighed. "It was probably a way of telling me he has found another girl. It is time for me to move on once and for all."

Modo couldn't help it. The words came out too quickly to stop. "Is he extraordinarily handsome?"

"He isn't a typical attractive man, but the way he treated me made me see him for who he really was." She set the cup down and dried her hands on her skirt. "The way you wield a sword reminded me of him. Please, can we stop talking about him? I'd rather focus on you."

It was ridiculous to be jealous of himself.

She had seen him, had loved him, even before he had been transformed, and straight-backed. But he was here, and *Quinn* was not.

"I'm sorry. I have no way of proving to you that I will not leave you, but I won't allow anything to come between us. If you dare give me your heart, I will treasure it for always." Modo pulled Bella up to a standing position and moved her away from prying ears and then whispered, "Because I love you."

# Chapter 34

# Bellarose

M odo said "I love you."

How could she not immediately give her heart to this man who so openly shared his? She had time, and yet it felt like the sands of an hourglass were slipping away quickly. Too many fates relied on her choices.

Bella gave him a gentle kiss on the lips. "I'm currently speechless and sweaty. I think I best go back to my room, take a bath, and mull over some things."

He chuckled. "I'm not laughing about the speechless part, but how open you are about the other. You never cease to surprise me. I don't expect a response until you are ready to give one. It is only that I didn't want any more time to pass before I told you my true feelings."

"We'll see each other at dinner?" Bella asked.

Modo beamed. "I'm looking forward to it."

Bella meandered back to her room in a daze.

Modo loved her.

Even Quinn had never said those words.

When Modo was snobbish and acted too prideful for his britches, she wouldn't have cared if he loved a fish. But now... Now to be loved by this man who saved her from a squall, and rescued her from captivity, who looked past her flaws, even if she was unsure if she could reciprocate. To be loved by a man like Captain Fitzwilliam Modo felt amazing.

If only Aerowyn would come back from the Kingdom of Magic and let her know if she discovered how Bella can help end all the hexes.

Her magical room must have helped her change into clean clothes, but she didn't notice. For now, she basked in the bliss of Modo's confession.

# Chapter 35

# Captain Modo

M odo looked forward to Bella's daily visits with him on the upper deck. Her endless curiosity amused him, especially since she unknowingly already knew the answers to her questions. Even so, he carefully left out details, so she wouldn't make the connections between him and Quinn.

"Where were you born?" She twisted her hair around her index finger.

"France."

She nodded. "I should have known that from your ship's name, but you have no accent." She squinted her eyes and asked, "Did you always want to be a ship's captain?"

He smiled and kept the answer succinct. "No."

She huffed. "Are you going to elaborate?"

"Maybe..." He winked. "Someday."

"If you can't trust me with significant details about your life," she huffed again, "how can we share one together?"

He quietly chuckled. "You don't need all the answers at once. This is beginning to feel like an inquisition."

"Then ask me some questions."

"Currently," he said with a smile, "I know everything I need to know."

"You told me that you love me," she whispered because there were men working nearby. "Doesn't that mean you want to spend your life with me?"

Modo touched her hand briefly. "Yes, but then that would mean we have a lifetime to get to know each other. Truthfully, I was hoping we could discuss that tonight after dinner. I know we've avoided being alone so you could decide your true feelings for me without all the kissing." He blushed but continued, "I think we need to be alone for me to be more transparent with you."

Bella tilted her head. "You don't want the crew to know about your past?"

"You could say that."

"I understand, but you promise to be more transparent with me?"

"I will try my best to appease your curiosity." Modo looked down. "Truly, I am not a very interesting person."

"Let me be the judge of that."

"Then meet me tonight under the stars where we practiced our swordsmanship—the place I told you I loved you."

"I will be there." Bella flushed, and a smile crept across her face. "And I know exactly what I will wear."

When he pressed her for details, she wouldn't even give a hint, but that evening after dinner, she arrived in a crimson gown. He was stunned.

He gulped, and she noticed, looked down, then peeped up through her lashes.

"You amaze me." He kissed her hand like a proper gentleman. "You remind me of a beautiful rose—Bellarose."

"Thank you. The color is a little bold, but as long as you think it looks like a rose, that was what I was hoping for."

She slid her hand into his. "The stars are so vivid this far above the ocean. During the day, the clouds and the sky create an illusion of the sea. Although," she added coquettishly, "most of my attention has been on a certain Captain Fitzwilliam Modo."

They gazed into each other's eyes, and he almost didn't notice as the lanterns grew fainter.

"Is it normally this cloudy at night?" Bella moved closer to him. "I haven't been on deck in the evening since the last time we were completely alone."

His attention darted to the railing. An eerie fog crawled across the deck, engulfing their bodies with misty air.

"No, this is strange." Goosebumps rose on his arms. The fog had a briny odor, but the ocean was too far away. It grew thicker, until he couldn't make out more than the faint blur of light from the lanterns. A familiar but difficult to place sound made him tighten his grip on Bella.

"Luckily, we're holding hands. I can't see—"

Bella disappeared from Modo's arms.

"Bella!" Modo cried. "Bella? Where are you?"

"I'm trap-ped," she gasped from his left.

Panic threatened to choke him.

A sharp thump shook the deck.

"Bella!"

The spine-chilling vapor evaporated, and a full moon illuminated what had happened to Bella.

Standing between Modo and the thick, black, spiked tentacles strangling Bella was Callista. Her eel-like body had grown legs, making her even more gruesome.

"Callista!" Modo reached for his sword. "What are you doing here?"

The sea witch cackled. "You didn't think you could keep me away by avoiding the ocean? I have magic too, and I used it to give us the ability to leave the water temporarily. Pixies are easily intimidated. I stole some dust and flew my kraken and myself here. My pet is currently wrapped around your ship. You aren't going anywhere."

Bella's eyes met his.

The kraken tightened its death-grip.

"Let her go!" He moved to puncture the hag with his sword, but her magic flared, forcing the weapon from his hand.

"No more delays." Callista snarled. "I tried kidnapping this girl to get Peter to change me back into my gorgeous self, but he has repeatedly ignored my more polite methods. Time to try something extreme."

Before Modo could draw his knife and charge at her, the sea witch slithered behind him. With uncanny speed, strength, and agility, she pushed his sword out of reach and shoved a knife against his throat. The witch overpowered him like he was a child.

Bella gasped, "Don't kill him!"

Callista bellowed in laughter. "Isn't that sweet? You want me to spare the other, without thought for your own lives. Should I kill you both, or let you decide?"

"You witch," Modo growled.

"Now, now, no name calling. You need to listen to my terms. I will free Bella if you tell her who you truly are."

Modo wriggled unsuccessfully to be free from the hag.

"She can live," Callista breathed in his ear, "but you will face something worse than death. Am I right?"

Slight pain notified Modo that the blade had cut the skin on his throat, and Bella's face paled in the moonlight.

"Or," Callista continued, "I could save Modo and not slit his throat if Bella takes on my curse and becomes the hideous sea serpent. Modo stays alive with all his secrets kept. I know in both scenarios neither of you have happy endings, but I don't care. I learned of Peter's ridiculous theory. Peter thinks he can reverse his spells when Bella finds happiness, but he is mistaken."

The kraken loosened his grip on Bella, but there was no way for her to escape, and that was all he wanted—Bella's escape. He needed to call out and tell her, but the knife at his throat made it difficult to speak.

"May I ask a few questions?" Bella's voice sounded small but defiant.

*"No,"* he mouthed.

Callista sniggered. "You may. How polite of you to ask, though I can't guarantee answers."

"How can you break your curse by switching with me? Aerowyn said curses couldn't be broken without sacrifice."

"Wouldn't that be a sacrifice for you to give up your humanity to save Modo? It worked when Gerard took Antoine's place."

Bella narrowed her eyes. "How did you know about Gerard?"

Modo found his voice. "Don't listen to her Bella!"

"Don't interrupt! Kraken, squeeze the prisoner."

The kraken obeyed and then sent more tentacles to pull Modo from the witch's arms and pin him to the deck railing.

"I know a lot about the fae and their injustices." Her captives secure, Callista stepped away from Modo. "When I wasn't getting results by kidnapping you or Modo, I decided I needed to dig into King Peter and Aerowyn's mysteries. I tortured some fae and merfolk with threats of worse fates than death to enlighten me, but no single creature knew all of what I needed. I even threatened Eira and gathered information from my spies who live on this ship and in New Orleans."

"Then I have but one more question," Bella said. "Who is Modo?"

The sea witch cackled. "That's for him to share. He has a choice; save you or risk something worse than death by revealing his secrets."

The kraken squeezed. There wasn't enough air to say more than, "No, Bella."

Her beautiful eyes locked onto his. "If I agree to switch with you, will Modo be safe? If he exposed his identity, would he be in any kind of physical danger?"

"Don't," he managed.

The beast's hold constricted around Modo, and for a moment, the world faded. Bella's heart-wrenching cry pulled him back.

"No! Please, let him live. I'll trade places with you. Let him go!"

Callista roared with laughter. "Oh my, that's priceless! No, you stupid, insignificant human. You can't negotiate the terms. You only have three options. First choice: you can both die. Second choice: you both live if he tells you who he is. Third choice: you both live if you take on my curse."

He wouldn't let her die. He couldn't let her take on that curse.

"Bella, I'm Quinn!"

The kraken released him, and he fell heavily to the deck. Modo's upper body began to slump, and deformed shoulder blades protruded. Quinn Modo howled in pain as his body tore through his shirt, and his face ached as his bones shifted.

Panting, he pushed himself up and stared at his old, familiar hands, then lifted his face to Bella's.

# Chapter 36

# Bellarose

Quinn was Modo, and Modo was Quinn?

Haze filled Bella's mind. She couldn't process what she was seeing, and yet—it made sense. Bella finally realized what her heart had tried to convince her mind for days.

How did she not recognize him? Modo fought exactly like Quinn had when teaching her to wield a sword. His phrases and expressions. His likes and dislikes. The way he knew her so well.

Her insides spun. She wanted to run to him and tell him she loved him, but the kraken kept her in place.

Quinn's frown contorted as if Bella's silence was affirmation of what Callista had assumed. The witch implied his true identity would cause him something worse than death and that was her rejection. Why else would he hide the truth from her?

"Sorry, Bella, I shouldn't have lied to you." His voice—the same but not the same from a different, twisted chest—sounded broken. "I thought you needed a handsome hero, not some deformed mutant. Aerowyn told me if I revealed my identity to you—"

"That you would go back to being Quinn." Bella finished the sentence for him. "But you don't understand. I love you, Quinn, just as you are. I tried not to when you didn't show up on the *Black Fear* to rescue me. I thought you didn't care enough for me."

Quinn lifted his head, and his chocolate-brown eyes held her gaze.

"This is too much!" Callista snapped. "She can't love you. You're hideous. Fine I'll force the fates."

Callista threw her knife into Quinn's chest. With a grunt, he fell over onto the deck. Bella's blood turned cold as his white shirt transformed to scarlet. She couldn't even scream.

"Here is my new bargain," Callista said. "I can save Quinn and repair his punctured heart, but you must make the sacrifice and take on my curse." She tapped her inhuman foot. "Now that I know you love that vile looking man, I believe you will."

"Bella—" Quinn wheezed. "Don't listen. You... love me... That is my happy... ending." He coughed up blood, then lay still.

"Quinn, don't die," Bella begged. "Let me kiss him and say goodbye!" Hot tears streamed down her cheeks. "I'll take on your curse if you allow me to say goodbye to him!"

Callista smirked and waved her hands around Quinn. The knife returned to her palm, his crimson shirt turned white again, and the bleeding stopped. He sat up as if nothing had pierced him. The sea monster released Bella, and she rushed to kneel at Quinn's side.

"Are you in a lot of pain?"

He caught her hands. "No, Bella you can't. You need to be free. Go, let me die."

"Oh, my Quinn," she whispered. "I love you."

"Can you really love... this?" He pointed to his bowed body. "Enough to lose your humanity?"

"There is more to anyone than their outer appearance. Your heart makes you the most handsome man I've ever seen."

He lightly wiped away her tears with fingertips lingering gently on her skin.

Their eyes met with intensity, and he whispered, "I'm willing to die a thousand times to hear those words."

He moved his hands to her waist and gently pulled her closer—brushing his lips over hers. Bella leaned into the motion. For the first time, Quinn's mouth—not Modo's—touched hers, and it was better than a library stacked with a million books.

"Bella, don't do it." He whispered against her skin. "Don't take her curse. You don't deserve it."

"I won't stop loving you," she murmured.

"Oh honestly. You two sicken me," Callista screeched. "You said goodbye, and now it's time to do what I want. Or I'll stab him again. Say the words."

Quinn and Bella clung to each other.

"Say it!" the sea witch demanded. "Say, 'I take on the curse of Callista forever.'"

Bella couldn't be brave if she held onto Quinn, so she released him and stood. She had her happily-ever-after knowing that Quinn loved her, and now she was willing to make the sacrifice for the man she loved. It had to be what would repair the twisted stories Peter and Aerowyn had broken. She knew it in the depths of her heart.

"I take on the curse of—"

A familiar voice called, "Stop, Bella!"

Golden light flooded the deck.

The flash illuminated a tall figure who stood between Callista and Bella. Her beautiful face was familiar, but her skin sparkled like stars. Platinum blonde hair gleamed in the moonlight, and a large black wolf stood proudly at her side.

"Aerowyn," Bella uttered.

Callista yowled. "You can't stop this. Quinn will die from the poison-dipped knife. I'll completely heal him if she goes through with this."

Aerowyn's eyes flickered as she regally announced, "Callista, I have a solution to fix your curse and all of the ones Father and I put upon this world. Seeing your behavior makes me doubt you deserve it, but I put the blame partially on my father for how he treated you."

"I was your sister's best friend." The sea witch ground her teeth. "Peter is fully responsible for taking away my joy and turning me into a sea monster!"

"I can take away your curse and save Quinn," Aerowyn said calmly.

Gerard whined as she spoke, as if he were pleading. A shiver crept down Bella's neck at the sound.

"Gerard, this is for the best." The enchantress stroked the wolf's massive head. "Trust me."

Callista glowered at them both. "Fine. I'm waiting, and Quinn will die if you don't hurry."

Aerowyn waved the golden scepter with a sun-shaped jeweled center on top. The vessel descended through the clouds. The ship rocked, and a huge wave of salt water splashed over the railings. Callista stumbled onto the boards on her unsteady legs. Bella held onto the deck rails, but Gerard and Aerowyn seemed to be motionless. Still seated, Quinn remained unmoved by the rapid descent.

The enchantress had brought the ship down from the sky. Callista's kraken withdrew its tentacles and disappeared from view as it escaped into the ocean. The sounds of feet and curses grew louder as most of the crew and rescued merfolk raced onto the upper deck.

"Beller!" Jeb shouted, "Are ya—"

Aerowyn swiped her wand over the crowd, and they all froze, as if time stood still. Then she turned to Callista, Bella, Quinn, and Gerard.

"Magic always comes with a price, and until recently, I felt there was no way to undo any of the damage. Thankfully, there is, and I will be able to do it."

"Enough of this spectacle and speeches. Get on with it." Callista glared. "Or Quinn will die!"

"What do you have to do?" Bella asked the enchantress.

"I simply give up my immortality and magic in this world. All my spells will reverse. Callista, I don't know if you will return to your former beautiful self since Father cursed you. I think most of the hexes I have cast will undo themselves."

The ship shook violently, and another flash of gold light temporarily blinded everyone.

A tall man with white-blond hair and shining skin appeared beside Aerowyn.

Callista reacted quickly to Peter's presence by hurling her knife at him, but he froze the object mid-air along with the sea witch. She became a statue with a sneered expression.

Peter touched Aerowyn's shoulder. "Daughter, you can't do this. You won't repair all the spells. Some of them were mine."

"I know, but I can help, and now that you are here, you can erase the memories of the crew and put them back where they belong. I won't be able to when I'm gone. Also, put this back in our ancestors' archives." Aerowyn placed the page into Peter's hand. "I tore it out of a book so Brynn and Aidan wouldn't try to stop me."

Peter frowned. "None of these people deserve mercy."

"This isn't how mercy works, Father. And, I won't die. I will simply live out my life in Bella's world. I will cast one more spell before giving up my powers that will ensure I become seventeen and live a normal life." Aerowyn put her hand on her father's arm. "You can visit me in the library I created for Bella, if you want. It will maintain the magic I weaved into it."

Bella blinked in confusion. Her library on the *Notre Dame*? Aerowyn had created it, but what did the enchantress mean about her 'world'? Yes, the strange flickers of dreams weren't from this realm, but surely, they were only the fanciful visions of a girl who read a lot.

"Daughter, that won't be enough for me. I risked everything to have a world with no hate or cruelty." Peter clenched his fists. "You can't undo it. Bella can rewrite the tales now that she is in love."

"You know that won't work. More stories will get twisted before she can finish, and then we'll never be able to undo all the wrongs we've created. This is for the best. It will be as if I were never here."

"I won't be able to forget you. I have already lost my wife and one daughter." Peter slumped. "Don't take my other child too."

"You could give up your immortality and join me when I'm Elayne. She doesn't have any parents."

Elayne? The name sounded familiar. Was that the girl Gerard had loved and lost?

Gerard whined. *I love you, Aerowyn.*

Aerowyn moved quickly to her father and hugged him, but—before anyone could speak—she pulled away and sang:

*I give up my immortality and magic now.*
*To reverse all the tragic, this I vow.*
*Make me seventeen once again.*
*To live my life as a human until the end.*

The smell of sulfur filled the air, and then it changed to pine, cloves, and oranges.

Bella, Aerowyn, Gerard, and Quinn stood in the middle of a large room full of tall shelves overflowing with books. Christmas decorations filled the room with their aromas of pine, cinnamon scented pinecones, and orange clove pomander balls.

A spiral staircase at the end of the room led to the second floor of bookshelves that encircled the library. The place looked familiar, yet Bella couldn't pull it out of her memory just yet. An aura of something otherworldly filled the room. Murals of fantastical creatures soared across the high, domed ceiling and moved as if live creatures were trapped inside each depiction. When a unicorn jumped out of one scene, a mermaid spiraled into it, the mythical creatures alternating at intervals.

In the center of the library, ornate yet cozy furniture—perfectly designed for comfortably hunkering down to read for a long time—encircled an open fireplace. A fully decorated Christmas tree was placed off to one side, and ladders with rollers leaned against the tallest bookcases, making the topmost, books accessible. A fat orange tabby cat added to the welcoming ambience of the room by appearing from nowhere, rubbing and weaving in and out of the groups' legs.

*Hobbes?* Why did Bella know the cat's name?

That wasn't the only difference, either. The whole group looked younger. Gerard was no longer a wolf. Quinn—she remembered now—had been reading the book she liked to read every December, *A Christmas Carol*, and when she'd told him that, he had offered to talk about it with her. He wasn't hunchbacked anymore. In Bella's opinion, his geeky glasses made him adorable. All four teenagers had dazed confused expressions, and they all began talking at the same time.

"Are you the enchantress or Elayne?" Gerard demanded.

"*You* were the egotistical war hero," Bella stated.

"And you!" Gerard turned to Quinn. "Didn't you have a humped back?"

Quinn focused on Bella. "What happened to your French accent?"

"Did that really happen?" Gerard rubbed his eyes.

"Have you always worn glasses?" Bella asked.

"Where are we?" Bella and Quinn questioned at the same time.

Gerard whistled with his index finger and thumb between his lips. The shrill sound shut everyone up. It also forced Bella out of the daze. She knew where she was prior to this.

"We can't all speak at once." He rubbed his temple. "I know all your names but was I in another world where you were different people. Elayne, are you also Aerowyn?"

"I prefer to be called Layney and I have no clue who Aerowyn is." Layney remarked, but when she averted her eyes, Bella couldn't help wondering if her friend was lying.

Gerard continued to stare at Layney.

"Do you know where we are and where we have been?"

She rolled her eyes. "Duh, we're in a library, and why are you only asking me?"

"I know this is a library." He narrowed his eyes at Layney. "But where does this library exist? What is this place?"

Bella held up her hands. "Wait. My memories are returning, and I *think* I know the answer. Layney led me to an old rickety Victorian house near our apartment complex. Am I right?"

Her friend nodded.

"Obviously," Bella continued, "the inside doesn't match the out-side because this room is pristine. You and Quinn followed us and then got magically sucked into the books with us."

Layney laughed a little nervously. "Bella, you're being ridiculous. I found this library over a year ago and fixed it up. We're in an old abandoned Victorian house that I pretend is a castle, but the books were left behind by the previous owners. With a lot of work, I turned it into my private oasis. I shared it with you since you like books and are new to our apartment complex. These two jerks have now made it less private."

Bella pursed her lips. The details Layney left out came into focus, but... maybe her new friend didn't want the interlopers to know everything?

"One, we're not jerks." Gerard scowled. "Two, Quinn likes books, so I'm sure it was his idea to follow you." He ran his fingers through his hair. "I can't remember."

"No, that's not correct," Quinn said tentatively. "Gerard thinks you're pretty and wanted to see where you were going. He forced me to tag along."

Gerard had been gawking at Layney, but at Quinn's remark, he turned to argue.

"I didn't say that. *You're* the one who thinks Bella is gorgeous. Brunettes aren't my type. I like blondes." He winked at Layney.

She blushed but put her hands on her hips. "Never-mind whose idea it was to follow us. Now you must keep this place a secret. I don't want anyone ruining it."

Bella couldn't help blurting out, "You all are remembering incorrectly. Layney is the enchantress who gave up her immortality and magic. She created this library for me to go in and fix all the fairy tales she and her father botched, but the only solution was for her to transform into a normal girl to repair the stories."

Layney and Gerard laughed, but Quinn seemed to be processing her words.

"Bella, did you hit your head? We only got here seconds before this. Look at my phone. The time hasn't changed." Layney pulled out her mobile phone and showed Bella the screen.

"You know I wasn't paying attention to the time when we came here," Bella argued. "So that proves nothing. Besides, if I'm delusional, how do you explain all the questions everyone was asking when we first arrived here? Gerard asked Quinn if he had a hunched back, and Quinn asked me why I didn't have a French accent."

Quinn cleared his throat. "We did have a bunch of strange questions only moments ago."

Gerard smirked. "If it was real, that means you two kissed."

Bella's cheeks warmed, but she turned to Gerard. "And that means you remember, too, *and* that you told Layney you loved her."

Gerard darted his eyes between Layney and Bella.

"You didn't hear those words come out of my mouth."

Bella nodded. "That's true. I heard your mind speak them."

"What are you talking about Bella? Gerard and Quinn got here right after us. How could you read his mind?" Layney squirmed. She was fibbing.

Gerard and Quinn glanced nervously at each other but said nothing. Maybe Gerard, the popular jock, was too cool to believe he got sucked into a magical book and had been turned into a wolf. Quinn was probably too sensible to accept anything so fantastical could have happened.

Layney, however, bit her lip, glanced at the boys, and crossed her arms. "Bella, you got so wrapped up in the story you were reading that you thought we were part of it."

"Wait," Bella protested. "Seconds ago, you said we just got here and showed me the time. How could I have read a book if we've only been here a few minutes?"

Quinn stepped forward and held up his wrist to show his watch. "She has a point, Layney."

"Did you pay attention to the time when you entered here?" Layney countered.

Quinn checked his timepiece. "What? That can't be. I checked the time to make sure I wouldn't be late for binging *Cobra Kai* with my dad before he went to work. He has an odd schedule."

"Nerd," Gerard whispered under his breath.

Bella scowled at Gerard. "I like that show. Does that make me a nerd too?"

He turned red. "I was only joking. I watch it too."

"So what time was it?" Bella asked Quinn.

"It was 10:00 when we followed you in, and now it is 10:02."

"See?" Layney waved one hand in the air. "We got here about two minutes ago."

Bella almost growled in frustration, but then an idea struck her. They'd have no choice but to acknowledge the truth. She smiled broadly. "Is anyone thirsty? I'm parched after that bike ride."

A glass of water floated in mid-air into Bella's open palm.

"No freakin' way!" Gerard exclaimed.

Bella beamed. "Try it. If your favorite treats are in one of these books, all you must do is ask."

He only hesitated a moment. "Can I get some grape soda and potato chips?"

A can of pop and bag of the salty snacks appeared in front of Gerard's face. He grabbed the can, plucked it open, guzzled it down, and belched.

"Disgusting!" Layney and Bella chorused.

Quinn's eyebrows drew together. "Does anyone find that disturbing?"

"Yes," Layney said emphatically. "He didn't have to burp so loudly."

"No, I mean that you two wished for something and it appeared from nowhere."

"Layney, out with it." Gerard looked fixedly at her. "Is Bella telling the truth?"

She sighed. "Of course, she's telling the truth."

Gerard flopped into one of the chairs. "I admit when I first opened my eyes to this room, I was afraid I was still a wolf."

"I thought I was going to have to lean forward due to my deformity," Quinn confessed.

Bella shook her head. "Then why did you two go along with Aer—I mean Layney?"

The boys shrugged their shoulders. Layney's mouth curved down and her shoulders sagged.

"What's wrong?" Bella asked.

"I..." Layney wrapped her arms around her body. "I'm alone. I lied about Layney having a father and aunt who live here. I also lied about living in the apartment complex so I could befriend you and take you to the fairy tales. I inserted some sketchy memories into Gerard and Quinn's heads so they thought they had known me for a long time."

"What does that mean for you now?" Bella asked softly.

Gerard and Quinn hovered around her.

"I can't go back to my father and all my magic is gone. All I have are these clothes and this phone I magicked before I lost all my abilities."

"You can live with me," Bella blurted out, then the questions hit. How could she explain any of this to her parents? They would call Social Services and get Layney into a foster home. Really, she would have hoped that if she had learned anything, it was to think before she spoke.

Layney shook her head. "That is asking too much."

Bella gave her friend a hug. "Then we'll be here for you. I bet we can use what we find in the library to fix up this house. You and I are both starting over. We'll find jobs and start high school together, and—"

"And we'll help," Quinn volunteered.

Gerard, however, only asked, "Layney, how old are you?"

"In this form, I'm seventeen, the same age as you. I will live my life as a mortal."

"I thought you said we'd eventually have our happy ending." Gerard stood up and reached for Layney's hand. "We'd ride off into the sunset—or some other kind of storybook nonsense."

Somehow, when Gerard spoke, Bella saw more than an arrogant teen. She also saw the war hero who sacrificed for his brother.

"You're human again and back home." Layney looked away. "Doesn't that make you happy?"

He shook his head. "No, the feelings were real. I still care for you. I won't be happy if you're not."

Tears welled up in Layney's eyes. "I care for you too. The moment you gave up your human life for Antoine, I couldn't help it. The truth is our adventures weren't only fiction. What you encountered was very real. The lives you met and touched were actual people. The magic of the library made time stand still in this realm, but we experienced all those things including the horrors of the war."

Bella stilled. Did that affect them here? Now?

Gerard's expression became somber. "Did I really kill all those British soldiers?"

"Yes."

"Was—" Quinn drew a deep breath "—was I really the son of that terrible man who beat me?"

Layney met his eyes, then looked away. "Yes."

"Are my parents alive here?" Bella whispered.

"Oh Bella," Layney said quickly. "Yes, of course they are! The ones who died on that ship from France were different people, even if they looked like your parents to you. That's how your mind worked out the time travel change."

The group stood quietly for a moment, as if they were replaying their quests.

Quinn eventually broke the silence. "Are we the same people? Obviously not physically for me. But did we really have those feelings?"

"Yes, you do really love Bella. I read your minds before I lost my fae abilities. All the feelings were real while you lived out the stories in these books." Elayne pointed to the shelves. "Once you returned to this realm, they returned to fairy tales."

Quinn's attention focused on Bella, and when he crossed the room and kissed her, she didn't mind at all.

He broke the kiss first and said, "Bella, if I hadn't met you in another world, I don't know if I would've had the courage to ask you on a date, but we've shared so much."

"Since it was real, and we were able to get to know the boy and girl we were and could be." She tucked her hand into his. "I'm glad I met you."

"I am too."

The room still had an unearthly glow that seemed to reflect Bella's inner warmth. Her heart swelled when Quinn flashed his signature half-smile. The horrible twists between the story world and real life evaporated into mist as the bright light of happiness burned it all away.

Somehow the grand adventure she had always longed for dulled when compared to the boy by her side. He had taught her to look beyond the superficial. She loved him, had even learned to love herself more because of it. No book—however detailed—could ever come close to the heart-stopping moments she had experienced in the fairy tale world. No story—however magnificent—could ever come close to the awe-inspiring emotions she experienced when Quinn proved that he loved her.

Bella leaned against Quinn's shoulder but looked at Layney. "Is this library still magical? Can time stand still when we read? Will we end up joining the stories?"

Layney's lips pursed. "Yes, even though I'm not a fae any longer, the things I enchanted in this world will always have their charms. That's why no one can know about this library. If we want to read here, we must bring our own books. We must never open any of the fictional manuscripts. It's too risky for any of us to return to that realm."

As irrational as it was, Bella's eyes welled up with tears. "So, we'll never know."

Quinn gave her a sideways hug. "Know what?"

"What happened. Did the stories repair themselves? Don't misunderstand," she added quickly. "I won't miss dangerous pirates and sea monsters, but I sort of will. I know the curses that Aerowyn—that you, Layney—cast will be reversed because of your sacrifice, but not all the hexes were your fault." Bella pointed to the shelves. "Will one of those books tell me if Eira goes back to being a human? Will Callista change her ways? If not, I hope she evaporates."

Gerard rubbed the back of his neck. "Did Brooke and Antoine get married? Did they ever wonder about me—us, I mean?"

"Or did they forget us, since we're no longer part of their world?" Bella turned to Layney. "What about Cerise and Jasper? Were they able to escape Callista, or did she set Jasper free once I wasn't there to help her?"

Layney's gaze fell. "I don't know. But you must promise not to go inside the stories. Our curiosity will have to be satiated by the tomes we buy or check out at the public library. We'll have to focus on old and new fairy tales to search for any mentions of those we've left behind. Anything else is too dangerous now." Layney's brows knitted together. "Without my fae abilities, the risk of jumping into books to check on them or on my... my father... is too great."

For a while, the only sound was the crackling of the fire.

Gerard kissed Layney on the forehead, and a box of tissues appeared to wipe teary eyes.

"The important question is," Gerard asked, "can we still get snacks from the non-fiction section?"

"Yes." The former enchantress grinned. "That, we can do."

Bella reached out and caught her friend's hand. "You've done so much to repair the damage, Aerowyn-Elayne-Layney. Your sacrifice is painful and beautiful. Love for Gerard, and love from all of us will hopefully make it worth it. I know that we will have our joyful conclusions like the fairy tales, but minus the magic."

And Bella believed that with her whole heart.

THE END

# Letter & About Author

*Dear Book Dragon,*

*Thank you for reading these tales. Rate, review, and tell anyone you can about my stories. Everything helps me continue writing. I've already begun drafting a stand-alone about Eira, the sassy dragon's background story. Bella wonders if her curse was broken. Do you? A total rewrite of my mermaid time traveling series is in the works too.*

*Always imagining, Carla*

## ABOUT

Carla Reighard lives with her husband and three cats, Han, Leia, and Kylo, who all attempt to "help" when she's crafting a new saga. Fairies, mermaids, talking animals, and supernatural bicycles were her childhood companions, but until the publication of *Elle's Magical Shoes*, they remained inside her head. If you're bold enough to read fairy tales and brave enough to believe in redemption, you've found the right book. See more of her work at https://carlareighard.com.

instagram.com/carlareighard/

goodreads.com/author/show/7085189.Carla_Reighard

facebook.com/people/Carla-Reighard/61567154826280/